WE
WERE
FLYING
TO
CHICAGO

STORIES
KEVIN CLOUTHER

Clouther

Published by Black Balloon Publishing
blackballoonpublishing.com

ISBN: 978-1-936787-15-9

Black Balloon Publishing titles are distributed to the trade by
Consortium Book Sales and Distribution
Phone: 800-283-3572 / SAN 631-760X

Library of Congress Control Number: 2013953124

Designed and composed by Christopher D Salyers • christopherdsalyers.com
Printed in Canada

9 8 7 6 5 4 3 2 1

WE
WERE
FLYING
TO
CHICAGO

STORIES
KEVIN CLOUTHER

BLACK BALLOON PUBLISHING
NEW YORK

These stories first appeared in the following publications, sometimes in slightly different forms: "The Third Prophet of Wyaconda" and "Charleston for Breakfast" in *Puerto del Sol*, "Isabelle and Colleen" in *The Gettysburg Review*, "Puritan Hotel, Boston" in *The Baltimore Review*, "On the Highway Near Fairfield, Connecticut" in *Gulf Coast*, and "Puritan Hotel, Barnstable" in *The Madison Review*.

For Ericka

TABLE OF CONTENTS

WE WERE FLYING TO CHICAGO

For no good reason, we were flying to Chicago. Our connecting flight had already left, and there was no hope of another that night. The flight attendant was a cruel sentinel. Stubbornly unattractive, she skulked in the corner, preemptively dismissing the complaints we all were thinking.

It goes without saying that every one of us hated her, and she hated every one of us. Once upon a time, men looked up from their newspapers and reports to notice her, but nobody did now, and for that she couldn't forgive us. We didn't blame her. We blamed the mute pilot. We blamed the pitiless thunderstorms. Mostly, we blamed Chicago. It was a city we had no interest in seeing. Nobody could even understand why we were going there. We had been tricked. It wasn't on the way. It was embarrassing. We didn't mention it.

More than most, the babies realized what was happening. They had no patience for such a pointless exercise. Their cries said, Explain your intentions! Youth is such an advantage. We felt overmatched. We buried ourselves deeper into the handheld devices we weren't supposed to be using. If the plane crashed, it would be our fault. The flight attendant had already implied as much.

Quietly, a woman began to cry. The woman's husband gripped her convulsing shoulders. He was grateful for the direction. An enormous man shuffling to the bathroom looked at them with soft recognition. He had held a woman this way, though not in many years.

"Her father just passed away," the husband whispered, but it wasn't true.

Earlier, the flight attendant had listed the enormous man's responsibilities. He was sitting in an exit row out of physical necessity. There were many responsibilities, and he wasn't listening to any of them.

"In the event of an accident, I am saving myself," he finally told her. "I am getting off this plane as soon as humanly possible and not looking back."

"So long as my directions are understood," the flight attendant said.

The in-flight magazine made the airports look like enormous spiders. That wasn't right, exactly, but there was something spidery about them. We landed in one leg, and the connecting flight took off in another. Not that it mattered. That plane would be gone by the time we arrived. When we deplaned we would go straight to the counter, where a tired woman would explain what we already knew: We had no plane. We would spend the night in Chicago. Unless the woman had left with our connecting flight. We didn't know what would happen then.

We didn't want to fight her. We recognized this wasn't her fault. There was only so much she controlled, but we had to blame somebody. The pilot wouldn't speak to us. Our calls—whenever we landed—would go unanswered. The flight attendant already hated us. We'd come to fear her. What would happen to us in Chicago? Would the flight attendant follow us to the hotel? If there was no woman at the counter, there would be no hotel. We'd camp in the terminal, our heads and legs dangling miserably from unmovable chairs. We were so uncomfortable already. We returned the magazine to the leathery pouch. Like everyone, we had been fascinated by kangaroos. As children, we dreamt of being carried in their warm pouches. It seemed a superior way to travel.

It wasn't long before the in-flight magazine was in our lap again. We traced blue parabolas from Los Angeles and Dallas and Atlanta to Chicago. We didn't know why Atlanta deserved so much attention. We couldn't name a single thing about Atlanta, outside of its sports teams. Outside of its having burned during the Civil War. We didn't know who burned it or why. Hadn't Chicago also burned? It used to be a different place. We couldn't help but think, somehow, that it was better before the fire.

Truthfully, we didn't like going anywhere. Flying had become so unpleasant. It wasn't just security. Everyone shared our complaints. It started with parking, which we didn't want to get into because someone wants to hear someone complain about parking? Who wants to hear someone complain about standing in line? Nobody, starting with us. We wanted a lot of things. To smoke cigarettes and not get emphysema. To eat baguettes and not get fat. To be where we were going and not Chicago.

The kids had the plastic trays down, and they were drawing. They were allowed to have the trays down because the plane wasn't moving. Most of them were drawing on paper, but some were drawing right on the tray. We didn't discourage it. Most drew planes in various stages of tragedy: yellow flames bursting from the wings, black smoke darkening an otherwise white sky. The windows were shrieking circles. We didn't ask questions. In fourth grade, the boys drew corporate logos between assignments in art class. The teacher, an unreformable hippie forced at gunpoint to serve in Laos, must have harbored grave fears about our generation. The boys drew outsized swooshes and colored them bright red. The boys wrote *NIKE AIR* and compared scripts. We fantasized about painting murals on school walls of heroic women slam-dunking basketballs.

When the plane finally took off, we put aside our anger. We tried to be grateful. The ground below us disappeared so quickly, but we didn't miss it. We were ready to move on to the next thing, even if that thing was Chicago. We could eat Chicago's hot dogs and drink its light beers. We didn't dislike Chicago because there was nothing to like. It was just that we didn't understand. The geography made no sense. It seemed wrong for the lake to lie east instead of north. Manhattan is surrounded by water, but Chicago is a grid that goes on and on until it grows tired. Just thinking of the streets exhausted us. We had a perverse desire to walk them until we collapsed. How high is the last number? We tried to guess. At least two hundred, maybe three. We imagined settling down on 300th street. We were a long way from anything we recognized. We couldn't see the Sears Tower. It didn't even feel like Chicago, which we appreciated. There was an abandoned lot across the street. Nobody could remember what used to be there. Behind the wild grass and sharp windows, we imagined a smoking factory. Something important was being made, so why shouldn't the city keep expanding? We had the space. Broad-shouldered immigrants could carry crates straight from the Mississippi to Lake Michigan. Everything the world needed would be, for a time, in Chicago.

The fact was we'd never been to Chicago. We'd seen Cubs games on cable and dark photographs in encyclopedias. The design of the Sears Tower also seemed wrong to us. Certainly, it was too disjointed for New York's sleek skyline. It didn't deserve to be taller than the Empire State Building. The Sears Tower wasn't even called the Sears Tower anymore, and that felt wrong too. We had no intentions of going to the top, even if it was allowed. Going to the top is always disappointing. If there's anything good about flying, it's the view. We could see everything we needed from the plane.

Would the lake really look like an ocean?
We read about kids in Harlem who had never seen
the ocean, who had no idea it was even there until an
enterprising teacher ushered them onto the D train, the
same train they took ten times a week. All it took was an
hour subway ride to the last stop. When the kids emerged,
the air smelled thicker. The birds looked different. People
were selling the same ridiculous junk and eating the same
disgusting food, but there was all of this blue. The kids
weren't inspired. They didn't look at each other with a wild
surmise. A few took pictures with their cell phones. One
yelled *shark*, and the rest laughed reluctantly.
We weren't sure what the point of that story was, what
it said about the younger generation or perhaps ours. We
weren't even sure the story was true. The flight attendant
pushed the drink tray down the aisle, and we ordered
ginger ale. She opened the can in front of us. The soda
made so much noise over the ice. We nearly told her the
story, but it wouldn't have made any sense.
Did you hear about these kids in Harlem?
I'm based in Charlotte.
Would you believe they'd never seen the ocean?
When I think of New York, I think of taxicabs and
Broadway and the Statue of Liberty. I don't think of the
ocean. I don't think anybody does.
We sipped ginger ale. From the scratched plastic
window, we saw miles of clouds. Anything could have been
below us. We could have been anywhere.

·

The closest we'd been to Chicago was Michigan. It was easy to love Michigan in the summer. It wasn't too hot, and there were lakes for when it was. Snakes slipped in and out of the lakes, which surprised us, but not in a way that discouraged us from hurling our bodies into the water. It was so cold before it was warm.

The boys were different, probably because we didn't know them. It was easy to imagine they were everything the boys from home were not. These boys were so easy to love! Their hair kept all the best things from the water. These boys were not at all concerned by the sun that clung to their naked shoulders. They didn't have to be handsome, which they realized. We knew they weren't this way around the girls they knew, but that didn't matter. We weren't this way around the boys we knew, either. It was one of those things that doesn't make any more sense, the more you think about it. We slept in open-windowed cabins. Our beds were so small and so hard. The sheets contained no softness. There were invisible insects everywhere. They zoomed up our nostrils and roared in our ears. We swatted at them unsuccessfully. We whispered conspiratorially about triumphs we were sure would never happen. We etched other people's initials into the wooden walls behind us. There were spearheads buried deep beneath us, but we didn't know how to reach them. We thought about treasure every time our bare feet shuffled across the dusty floor. We were desperate to remove the floorboards and make important discoveries. Crickets called to each other until we fell asleep, and in the morning, tiny birds filled the trees above our pillows.

We learned archery, but our successes were random. Aiming had little effect on the weapon's trajectory. We learned to start fires and patch leaking canoes. Everything in our backpacks was essential. We were more interested in the narrow forest around us. It seemed fitting that danger should lurk there. We imagined limping men with weapons more powerful than arrows and pocketknives. It was important that the men have several attractive victims. We were required to learn the names of every tree in the forest, and even today, we find ourselves silently going through them in the midst of some mindless errand. We don't know our husbands' phone numbers by heart, but we can list every tree in Blue Lake, Michigan.

We tried to guess where we were. Our seats were over the wing. We were always over the wing, which we hated, which we blamed unreasonably on the website we used to select our seats. We didn't remember choosing such terrifying seats. A green light blinked at the end of the wing. The light didn't even look attached to the plane. We imagined a green monster crawling the length of the wing, tapping its scaly fingers against our thick window. We tapped back.

We tried to determine what kind of monster. It was important that the monster be small. More frightening that way. More likely to inflict the proper amount of fear. We tried to make the monster frightening, but our imagination was so poor. Everything we imagined was limited to the movies we'd watched as kids. We wished it were otherwise. We tried to construct, from the unwieldy limbs of our memories, a monster more frightening than the ugliest demons we'd seen. It didn't do any good. We kept seeing gremlins. We kept seeing zombies with hockey masks and manicured dead men.

The kids were better. It was nothing to these children to color the sky green. We saw that sky one summer in Michigan, though not the tornado that followed. For that, we were underground. We hadn't realized the space existed. There were no windows, so nobody took the danger seriously. The room was filled with soft boxes leaking ancient issues of *National Geographic*. The borders were barely yellow. The natives looked more sad than restless. We wanted to spare them from whatever misfortune they'd been born into, but we were only children, and they were older than their pictures anyhow. We believed we were capable of great charity then, that anyone would want our help. Now we missed that feeling. Now we couldn't help anyone. We pictured our own outsized heads framed in yellow. We didn't dare guess the headline.

We wondered why we never saw other planes. Why we never saw helicopters or even birds. Certainly not flying saucers, which we were desperate to believe in for reasons we had a difficult time explaining. On a flying saucer, at least, we wouldn't have to worry about sitting over the wing. Thousands of feet in the air with nothing else in sight, we only had ourselves to blame. We could have stayed. When we were younger, we didn't see the point in living anywhere but Blue Lake. There our shames were private, and people liked us for the way we talked and what we did. Weren't we saying and doing good things?

We were happy. It wasn't hard. The world didn't have to be hard. Nobody could convince us we were wrong.

Big-hearted counselors, open your arms. More than ever, we need your warmth. We didn't mean for it to go this way. Promise us you'll never age. Promise us you'll never stop being wise, tall, confident, an excellent shot. Remember the best things about us. There was no reason to dislike us then, beyond our capacity for misery, but what did we know about that future? What did any of us know about anything, past what we could see in black cabins, deep in the woods, trembling with joy beneath the breathing of sleeping strangers?

The initial descent was rocky. The air turned warm. We felt like we were about to be sick. We unfolded the bag behind the in-flight magazine. We hadn't realized they still made these bags. It made us even more nauseated. We looked around to confirm everyone felt as sick as we did. The lights flickered before turning off completely. We waited for the pilot to deliver terrible news, but the speakers were silent, and the flight attendant sat calmly. If anything, the flight attendant looked a little bored. She looked like she could use a cigarette. We could use one. We wanted to like her.

The plane felt like a roller coaster. That might not be an original comparison, but it's what the plane felt like. We imagined a giant track in the sky. We imagined stoned teenagers pulling levers below us. The metal square of the seat belt pushed into our bloated abdomens. The little nozzles that spray cool air didn't spray anything, and we

were so hot. We fanned ourselves with the magazine. The
babies started crying again, and we didn't blame them.
We considered crying, but what would that look like? We
told ourselves we couldn't be crashing and looked out the
window like we weren't even looking. It was too dark to
read anyone else's panic. Even the flight attendant had
gone invisible. We missed her.

The landing surprised us. We weren't sure why. The
plane had to land eventually, but in the air, we had no
understanding of time. We didn't even have watches. We
just had phones, which we were desperate to check. From
the runway, Chicago looked like another cloud. This cloud
was darker, like it wanted to rain, only we were on the
ground with nothing but asphalt in every direction.

There are two airports in Chicago, but we didn't know
at which one we landed, or whether it mattered. The pilot
said we were taxiing. Why had we never heard of a taxi
taxiing? Our phones were full of messages from people
we didn't want to talk to, people who didn't even like us.
We still wanted bread. We always wanted cigarettes. We
didn't want to be reasonable anymore and we didn't want
to be in Chicago.

In New York there had been a young woman waiting by
security, her neck held up with colorful scarves. Everyone in
line adjusted, as if to make room for her beauty. No matter
how vapid we become, how senseless our days grow, these
girls still arrive at airports, as hopeful as they've ever been.
We should mention that some of us had been these girls.
We applied red, red lipstick. The skin around our eyes was

so smooth, but we didn't think about it. We thought about which skirt went with which blouse and which jewelry— our jewelry was so cheap—and we weren't dressing for anyone. We were dressing for the thrill of being young, though we didn't call it that. We didn't call it anything. That would come later. Most things would come later. Then we could live on anticipation. Some mornings, we leapt out of bed. Nothing hurt, so we felt it all. We couldn't wait to meet our boyfriends, go to class, read everything. Chicago sounded like a magnificent place to visit.

THE THIRD PROPHET OF WYACONDA

Henry Alexander wasn't the first person in Wyaconda, Iowa, to spend time as Jesus. Before him had been Bill Boucher, in the mid-1980s, who maintained that the Holy Ghost came to him at the Texaco station on Main Street. Before him there was Ezekiel Wood, at the end of the nineteenth century, who, in spite of his Biblical name, ultimately decided that the responsibilities of being the Messiah were incompatible with his gambling habits.

Wyaconda is a town of fewer than a thousand people, and although almost everyone is a practicing Christian, there isn't anything especially religious about the place. The town is situated on the South Wyaconda River, just north of the Missouri border and an hour's drive from the Mississippi. It was founded in 1859 by a fur trader who'd wandered southwest from Quebec. Not much is known about the man, but school children still learn the alphabet in English and French, and for six years in the 1970s, the sign leading into town read *Welcome to Wyaconda, The Montreal of the Midwest.*

Henry never actually claimed to be Jesus. That part was a misunderstanding. Henry had only said that he was a prophet. Not Jesus, but in the grand holy tradition of Jesus. A prophet, most everyone agreed, was more acceptable. So a week after his arrival, Henry took to preaching every morning from nine until noon to spread his word. To avoid further confusion, he spoke as specifically as possible.

"I have spoken to the Lord, and the Lord will be among us soon." Henry wiped his forehead with the back of his hand. "The Lord is not pleased."

Henry was standing in front of Cal's barbershop on Main. Since it was summer, there were kids sitting on the sidewalk with nothing better to do.

"Where'd you talk to the Lord?" a boy with white hair asked.

"Why—" Henry stuttered. "Where do you *think* I talked to the Lord?"

The boy hadn't been expecting to answer any questions and he was more honest than he normally would have been. "Des Moines," he said.

"Des Moines?"

"Des Moines is the capital." The boy thought he might not know.

"The Lord spoke to my soul, son. Do you know what a *soul* is?" But Henry saw that the boy was done answering questions, so Henry kept talking. "The Lord came into my soul and said the world has become a dangerous place. He said the kingdom of Heaven has come near."

"What does the Lord sound like?" a girl asked.

Henry kneeled, as if to tie his shoes, but looked toward the sky instead. The children watched him intently. They weren't allowed to ask these kinds of questions in Sunday school.

Henry said, "You mustn't think of the Lord as being like you or me."

But this was something the children had heard before, and they began to lose interest. Two boys ran up screaming about a frog, and before long most of the children had left. Shortly thereafter, Megan Pullman appeared, looking for her son. He was late for lunch.

"Have you seen my Scottie?" she asked.

"I've seen children, ma'am, but I don't know if I've seen Scottie."

"He's got a cut on his elbow and he's wearing an orange shirt."

"If you listen, if you have just ten minutes to listen, I can tell you about the Book of Matthew. It is a beautiful book, I promise."

Henry leaned in and touched Megan's arm. She didn't like being touched by someone she didn't know, but it was a brief, awkward touch, and it made him seem more sincere. And although she was uninterested in what Henry had to say—she had a church, after all—she liked that he'd asked her. Scottie was late, it seemed, every other day. When you thought about it, what was ten minutes?

"Go on," she said. "Tell me."

Nobody knew where Henry Alexander came from. When pressed he would demur, though that didn't keep people from developing theories. In the rhythms of his voice, some detected a slight Southern accent, and to more than one person, his clothes suggested New England. After listening to a Thursday sermon for nearly two hours, Reverend Gregory walked home with his hands in his pockets and told his wife that Henry was almost certainly a European.

The first thing Henry did when he arrived in Wyaconda was take a room in Mrs. Speers's boarding house. Mrs. Speers was a widow in her fifties who'd run all six units by herself since her husband's death. When Henry arrived with one small suitcase and a framed three-foot tall John the Baptist painting, she assumed he wouldn't be there long. Henry didn't have a driver's license, or even an identification card, but he paid in cash, and Mrs. Speers wasn't particular about tenants who paid that way.

At first Henry preached in front of Cal's seven days a week, but after a couple of weeks, he started taking off Sundays. Leave the Lord's Day to the Reverend, he told Mrs. Speers, and many were surprised. There were those who assumed that Henry Alexander and Reverend Gregory weren't compatible, that Wyaconda wasn't big enough for the two of them. But neither man had much of a problem with the other. The way Henry talked about it, they were both in the same business. The way Reverend Gregory put it, Henry was harmless.

The person who did develop a grievance with Henry was Cal, who'd been running his barbershop without distraction for twenty-five years. At first Cal didn't mind Henry, but when he witnessed a young mother and her son walk away from the barbershop because of Henry's preaching, Cal stormed out the front door and confronted the prophet.

"What do you think you're doing?" Cal said.

"Sir, I'm here to do the Lord's work."

"So why do you have to do it in front of my barbershop?"

Henry stepped back. Cal was a reasonable man. He considered himself a good barber, husband, and father. There were only two things that set off his temper: One was his eldest son, and the other was people he didn't understand. Henry Alexander seemed like a man Cal would never understand.

"I'm going to ask you to leave my premises. I'm going to ask you once nicely—"

"You don't have to ask me twice."

"That's good."

"Because I'm not leaving."

It was at this point that Cal took his first long look at Henry, and like so many before Cal, he was surprised at what he saw. Maybe it was the black—black pants, shoes, shirt, hair—or maybe it was the constant gesturing, but people assumed that Henry was an ordinary-sized man, when he was anything but. He looked about thirty, was well over six feet tall, and close to 250 pounds. He wasn't fat—the weight was distributed democratically across his body—but he wasn't muscular, either. He was simply large. When he stepped forward so that his face was only inches from Cal's, it was clear that he was serious.

"The Lord has asked me to do my work here."

Land is flat along the Wyaconda River, and sound there runs quick and close to the ground. When Cal walked back into his barbershop, you could hear the bronze bells above his door clear down Main Street.

Every morning Henry Alexander did the Lord's work in front of Cal's barbershop, but when summer ended and the children went back to school, there were mornings when not a single person would stand and listen. It may have been Main Street, but Wyaconda is a small town. Besides the barbershop, there was a bank, a Mexican restaurant, a post office, a gas station, and an abandoned gas station. There were other stores, too, but they opened and closed so irregularly, nobody bothered to keep track of what was there and what wasn't. Some days Henry would deliver his sermon to an empty road, step into the gas station at noon for a soda, and head back to the boarding house. When Mrs. Speers asked him if it bothered him that no one was listening, he paused and then said, "They hear me."

People heard Henry, that was true, but it was difficult to say if they ever carried a thought from his mouth to their homes. People didn't know what to do with him. They'd seen evangelists on television, and in the bright lights and swooning, religion was put on stage in a way that it never was on Sunday mornings. And although those shows disturbed them, they were exhilarating in a way that Henry's speeches never were. To an extent, people wanted to be scared by Henry. Because Henry had come so suddenly and he was so large and there really was no good reason for any of it. But Henry never pretended he was there to please anyone, and that was part of the problem. There was no element of entertainment in his performance. It wasn't even a performance. He was too genuine.

If Henry failed to move the town it was not from lack of effort. After the first hour or so of preaching, he began to sweat, and the sweat continued, coming in dark and heavy around his shoulders and down his back, shining on his bare arms, and beading into a crown beneath his hair. His voice cracked, and his blue eyes sharpened so that even if he was looking straight at you, he wasn't really looking at you because he was looking *past* you, looking at something you most certainly would never be able to see. It was an intimidating look, even inspiring, but Henry looked so hard he forgot his preaching and began to trail off. He treaded water with this or that parable, but soon enough he was completely incomprehensible, and anyone who had been listening walked away. Then Henry scratched his stomach, baffled as the next person, and picked up fresh from a different part of the New Testament. That lack of focus, Mrs. Speers told him, wasn't a good quality for a prophet.

For a prophet, Henry didn't prophesize all that much. Mostly, he talked about the Lord. A retired veteran tried to get him to predict the weather once, but Henry called it a misappropriation of the Lord's vision. It was little things like that—not taking the easy road—that made people not mind his being around.

Of course, that was before the baptizing started.

Mrs. Speers said the three-foot tall painting of John the Baptist should have been a hint. That's what prophets do, she said. They baptize.

Henry had started small, baptizing tree branches and scrap metal. At noon, he would walk the half mile to the Wyaconda River, remove his black shoes and socks, and wade waist deep into the water with a piece of aluminum siding or oak. Reverend Gregory walked along the river after lunch some days, and he saw it first. The baptisms went on for five or six days in a row, but Henry could never finish the task. It wasn't that he didn't know the words, or that he had bad form, only that he seemed, ultimately, reluctant to push anything underwater.

Henry declared himself ready for baptism the next Monday. He was in front of Cal's a half-hour early, calling for volunteers.

"What if you've already been baptized?" Megan Pullman asked. She was walking her dog.

"That depends if you're ready to welcome the Lord into your life."

"And if I am?"

"Then I'll baptize you."

"And if I'm not?"

Henry bent his arms back and opened his mouth, though no words came out. Megan looked down uncomfortably, and the dog, a heavy German shepherd, walked over and licked Henry's fingers.

"What do you think, Moose?" she asked.

"I don't think the animal has an opinion. This is your soul we're talking about."

"He's a very sensitive dog." Megan pulled on the dog's collar, and it jerked back in surprise. Reluctantly, the dog followed her down the street.

Henry continued his preaching for the rest of the day, but nobody stepped forward for baptism. When Henry arrived at the barbershop the next morning, Cal's son Jeffrey was pacing up and down the street, calling for his cat. Jeffrey had dropped out of high school earlier in the year, though this was something Cal did not know.

"Son, you look like someone in need of help."

"I've been coming down for months."

"I can see that."

"Maybe a year."

Jeffrey's hair was tufted up in different directions, and his pupils were larger than they should have been. He'd forgotten to take the pills he bought in Cedar Rapids with water, and there had been a chalky taste in his throat for the past three hours.

"I'm here to offer you salvation."

"I'd like to lie down."

"Will you come with me? Will you do that for yourself?"

Because Jeffrey had nowhere else to go, he said yes. For the occasion of his new baptism, Henry bought him a juice from the gas station. By the time they reached the river, Jeffrey was certain he was about to be killed.

"I don't think I want to be baptized anymore."

"I cannot force the Lord on anyone."

"I'll pay you for the juice later. I'm good for it."

Henry scratched the back of his neck and looked at the river. It was a thin part of the river, no more than thirty or forty feet wide. There wasn't much of a current. While Henry looked at the river, Jeffrey slowly began to walk backward. He had a terrible headache, but he figured everything would hurt less once he was consumed with the physical process of running.

"I don't mean you any harm." Henry still had his back to him.

"What's—"

"I brought you here because the Lord asked me to do his work. In that way, I'm no different from your reverend, except that I see things. I didn't ask for any of it."

"My father doesn't like the preaching. He says it's bad for the shop."

"Cal is your father?"

Jeffrey continued to walk backward, his eyes fixed on Henry's back. If Henry moved quickly, he was prepared to run. He had been on the track team long enough to learn how far he could go before his body gave out.

"You see things. What do you see?"

"I see that the kingdom of Heaven has come near."

"Can you do things? Can you walk on water?"

"No."

"You shouldn't bring people out here. It's creepy." He waited to see if Henry would turn around.

"If I were a better prophet, if I had the right words, you

wouldn't wonder. I could make you see, and you wouldn't wonder."

Jeffrey didn't know how to respond to that, and he figured it would be best if he walked away quietly. It wasn't until he was out of Henry's sight that he started running.

Reverend Gregory had been content to dismiss Henry, but when the whispers grew loud on the church steps after service, the reverend took notice. Henry hadn't managed to baptize anyone, but his persistent offers had begun to worry certain parishioners. Most people thought he was innocent enough—a little crazy, perhaps, but not dangerous. There were those, though, who'd shifted their view since Jeffrey's encounter. They wanted Henry out of Wyaconda, and the more people talked, the more the reverend became concerned.

Reverend Gregory considered approaching Henry, but every time he saw him on Main Street, Henry was engaged in conversation with someone. On a couple of occasions, the reverend had allowed himself to listen, and he had been taken not with the sincerity of Henry's words, but with his persistence. Depending on whom he was speaking to, Henry's rhetoric would shift, though the message remained consistent: I have been called to speak for the Lord, and the Lord is coming soon. It made the reverend wonder about his own preaching, about how well he communicated the Gospel to his parish. He was thirty-nine years old and had reached the point where he rarely questioned his calling. But his effectiveness, that was something different. Did people attend his services because they had to, or were there those who were genuinely moved by his words, who sought real guidance from his regular presence? He didn't know the answer, though it seemed as important as any question he'd ever asked himself, even the one of his calling.

The importance of that question finally brought the reverend to Henry. Reverend Gregory had seen nothing on his own to make him question Henry's harmlessness, but he considered it his responsibility as leader of the parish to confront him regardless. Just to be certain. So one day while Henry was speaking to the Walkers, a middle-aged couple from the parish, Reverend Gregory joined their small circle with a quiet nod of the head.

"I was speaking about a vision I had," Henry said to the reverend. "One man of God to another, I'll be honest. I'm very scared."

Mrs. Walker nodded, and her husband smiled. Her earnestness amused him.

"What did you see?" Mr. Walker asked.

"The Lord came to me in my sleep, but I did not see His face. Before Him, there was a wall of angels, blond and a mile wide. My mind was trimmed with blue-white clouds." Henry pulled out a handkerchief and dabbed it across his face, though it was not warm outside. "I said, 'Lord, what do I do?' and He said, 'Tell them. Show them.'"

Henry pushed out his arms and held his hands before him. Mrs. Walker leaned forward to inspect the giant bare palms.

"I don't understand," she said.

"There's nothing to understand," Mr. Walker said.

"There's nothing." And with that he walked away.

"You'll have to explain this to us later," Mrs. Walker said solemnly.

"It's all a matter of perception." Henry turned to the reverend. "I meant what I said before. I'm scared."

"Henry, there is a lot to explain," the reverend said, already angry with himself for starting harshly. "There are people, a number of people in my parish, who are concerned."

Henry sighed. "Can we discuss this, maybe over lunch?"

The two men wished Mrs. Walker farewell and walked to the gas station. The station had four pumps and a small store. What was called *the deli*—a makeshift counter where you could order ham or turkey sandwiches—was an addition the reverend wasn't familiar with. When Henry said *lunch* and headed toward the gas station, the reverend thought candy bar, or, at best, apple pie in a green wrapper.

"People are worried about the baptisms," Reverend Gregory said, as Henry ordered. "Everyone in the parish has already been baptized."

"But not everyone in the town."

"No, but everyone in the parish, and the makeup of the parish is very close to the makeup of the town."

"How many times have you been baptized, Reverend?"

"Once, of course."

"Me, three times. The third time was the charm." Henry handed the reverend a sloppy turkey sandwich on a paper plate. "Look, it's a restaurant now."

"My parishioners do not wish to be baptized again."

"I'm sympathetic to that, Reverend, but I'm following

a higher order here. May I be frank? May I be frank in telling you that there is going to be a miracle?"

Henry raised his eyebrows and took a ferocious bite from his ham sandwich. When he swallowed, half the sandwich was gone.

"You're the first person I've told, but by the end of the month, everyone will know. They'll see for themselves."

"A miracle?"

"I'm scared too, Reverend, but the Lord has willed it."

The reverend fingered the bread of his turkey sandwich. People in the gas station had begun to look at them, and he, in turn, had become conscious of their slightest movements.

"A miracle," he repeated. "Yes, that would be something." He gently placed his plate on the counter and nodded goodbye before heading toward the door of the station.

Soon the miracle was all anyone in Wyaconda could talk about. A gossipy parishioner had overheard the reverend tell a visiting clergy member about it, and that was that. The conversation may as well have been posted on the front door of the church itself, such was the way news spread in a town of fewer than a thousand people.

Nobody believed the miracle would happen because everyone had come to understand that miracles were of a different time and place, the stuff of mountains in the Middle East. Besides, what had Henry Alexander ever done to make a person believe he was capable of foreseeing something as grand as a miracle? It was too much even to think about. Mrs. Speers, who had taken some Latin, said that for the Romans, the word meant *to wonder*. She didn't believe in the miracle any more than anyone else, but she especially wanted it to happen, remembering the good things bestowed upon those in the bible who housed prophets and saints and angels.

But what if it did happen? You couldn't help but entertain the thought, even if only for a second. Because if it did happen, it would have to be something inexplicable, and what would that something be? The instinct was to guess, to put a name to the unnameable, and all across Wyaconda that's precisely what people did. At the bar after work, men gathered to talk about what a miracle meant. Soon enough they had a mock pool, with each man picking the day it would happen and what it would be. There was no money involved, but when two men guessed the same thing—that they would live forever—there was a heated argument before the bartender clarified that it didn't matter, that so long as each man picked a different day, there could be a clear winner.

Old women talked in whispers at the market, and in the schools, the older children had their own guesses. Jeffrey even returned to class, finding that his near baptism afforded him a sort of celebrity status. For those serious about the matter, though, the preferred locale was Cal's barbershop, where one overly curious man took to getting haircuts daily, so as to justify his continuous presence. It was generally agreed that if the miracle that most certainly was not going to occur were to occur, it would happen in front of Cal's barbershop. So Cal came to shift his opinion

of Henry Alexander once more, deciding that even if the
man had tried to baptize his son, it was good business
having him around.

All this attention was not lost on Henry, who brought
a new reverence to his sermons. At the end of the morning,
he found himself no less soaked in sweat, though he rarely
trailed off mid-speech, or lost his attention gazing beyond
his audience. Each day he limited himself to one or two
passages from the Gospels, and while his thoughts jumped
from one idea to another, the transitions were there. You
could follow him; logically, it made sense. The weather
had cooled to the point where Henry added a white coat
to his otherwise black uniform, and there was something
dazzling about this last piece of clothing, not just in the
way that it clashed, but also in the way that it fit, in the
way that it seemed it belonged all along. Everyone was
desperate for a miracle. But while they were waiting,
people were content to gather from time to time and listen,
to make space for an enormous blue-eyed man to tell them
kindly about the end of the world.

Then a funny thing happened: Henry stopped giving
sermons. Megan Pullman said that his most recent one
had been only mediocre, and people talked about what a
shame it would be if it was his last. So the rumor spread
that he was preparing. That the miracle was due any day,
and that Henry was working around the clock to ready
himself.

When Henry showed up again at the barbershop, three
days after his last sermon, the only person there was Cal. It

had been raining all morning, and Cal could barely make out Henry's form—dark and waterlogged—through the thin fog of the barbershop window.

"Nothing worse than cold rain," Cal said, pushing the door open with his arm.

"Rain began in the mind of the Lord," Henry said.

"That's one way of saying it."

Henry nodded, as if to show it was a small point they could agree on.

"It's wet out there. You want to come inside?"

"I heard the reverend's getting his hair cut today, and I thought maybe I could talk to him."

"We'll see about all that," Cal said, knowing the reverend got his hair cut the third Friday of every month and realizing Henry knew that, too.

The barbershop seemed smaller with Henry in the corner, and it suddenly occurred to Cal that in all the months Henry had been preaching outside his door, he'd never once stepped inside. It made him wonder where Henry got his hair cut. For an hour, Henry sat in a chair in the corner with his hands folded over his lap, and Cal didn't have two words to say to him. The storm struck Cal as an omen, and soon enough he found himself searching for clues in the clumps of cut hair spreading on the wet floor tile. When the reverend finally did enter, he found the barbershop strangely quiet, what with Cal staring at the ground, and Henry so still in the corner.

"Gentlemen," the reverend said, hanging up his rain slicker. "Is everything all right?"

"About the miracle," Henry said.

"The miracle—"

"It's happening tonight. I thought I should tell you first."

Reverend Gregory left his hand on the slicker. "Henry, there is nothing dishonorable in stepping away from all this."

"It's happening here."

"God is concerned only with the truth."

"Every tree that does not bear good fruit is cut down and thrown into the fire." Henry stood. "You'll see, Reverend."

The reverend looked toward Cal, who leaned back against the counter and turned his head. The counter was littered with the tools particular to a barber: razors, mirrors, combs. Reverend Gregory wished only to sit in the elevated chair and have Cal spread a white cloth across his chest, to close his eyes and listen to the precise, regular clicks of the scissors. The reverend didn't let Cal put an electric razor to his hair, except in the back where he squared it at the neck. It was an unspoken understanding between the two men but it was remembered unfailingly, and Reverend Gregory appreciated this.

"I think the reverend came for his haircut," Cal said. "Reverend, is that right?"

"Yes."

"So perhaps it would be best if you conducted your business with the reverend after his haircut. If that's all right with you, Reverend?"

"Yes, of course."

Henry nodded slowly. "You will know me by my fruits.

Just please remember the miracle. Thank you."

Both men smiled, and Henry walked out the door.
A steady rain was still coming down. Reverend Gregory
climbed into the chair, and Cal removed the reverend's
glasses. Cal began to say something, but noticing the
reverend's eyes were already closed, he thought better of it
and moved to the sink to wet his comb.

Henry told Reverend Gregory about the miracle first, but
he didn't end there. All morning and into the afternoon
Henry walked up and down Main Street in the rain,
announcing the time and place of the miracle. Then when
the rain stopped, as if on cue, Henry walked away without
a word. By evening, all of Wyaconda knew. People had
their excuses for coming—It's such a nice night, they said,
It'll be good to see everyone—but ultimately, everyone
came for the same reason. After all, how many chances
does one have in a lifetime to see a miracle?

They came with blankets and sweaters. They came with
pitchers of lemonade and flash cameras. Reverend Gregory
came and so did Cal. Were it not for the changing foliage
and autumn air, it could have been the Fourth of July. The
children were fooled like flowers in a warm winter. They
looked up to the night sky patiently, expecting it at any
moment to crack open with color and light.

The Walkers arrived late and set up their chairs on
the sidewalk opposite Cal's barbershop. The best spots
were directly in front of Cal's, but they hadn't arrived early
enough to get them. To their right, a mother was lowering
sandwiches out of a picnic basket, and to their left, a young

man was scribbling furtively in a palm-sized notebook.

"I don't really expect anything," Mrs. Walker said.

"What's there to expect?" Mr. Walker said. "It's just another night is all."

A group of girls playing tag swarmed into the street. They spread into a circle and eyed each other suspiciously, their elbows bent and hands floating by their hips, as if ready to pull a pistol.

"The reverend is here, you know," she said.

"Everyone is here."

"I know, but the reverend."

Mr. Walker shifted in his chair and scanned the crowd for the reverend. He couldn't find him. Mr. Walker said, "It is a bit strange."

"That the reverend's here?"

"That any of us are here."

A game of touch football had started under the two streetlights that still worked. Mr. Walker looked toward the game and then toward his wife. A light wind moved through everyone's hair on its way to the trees behind Main Street.

"I didn't even think not to come," he said.

"Why would you?"

"It's not going to happen. I know that. But I'm here."

"Everyone is here. You said it yourself."

"Imagine that? I didn't even think not to come!"

An hour later people began to leave. Two hours later it was too late for most of the children to be out, and three hours later nearly everyone else decided it had been long enough. Cal locked up the barbershop then—

he'd left it open to sell cookies his wife had made that afternoon—and Mrs. Speers left too, promising she hadn't seen Henry all day. By midnight, just a few young people were left along Main Street, mostly because the miracle had presented an opportunity for them to drink and flirt with each other. When they left, only Reverend Gregory remained. He sat alone on the sidewalk until sunrise, tapping his finger on a small crimson Bible and asking the Lord to lend him strength through a time he did not understand.

For months there was speculation as to where Henry had gone and why. There were those who figured he'd taken 63 south to some small town in Missouri, and others who were sure he'd taken 34 west to Nebraska. One man said he saw Henry with a beard and young wife in Cedar Rapids, and another man promised he'd seen Henry dealing blackjack on a riverboat on the Mississippi. A ten-year-old girl raised eyebrows upon claiming to have witnessed his sudden and dramatic ascension into Heaven. When Reverend Gregory asked her why she thought the Lord had taken Henry, she suggested that maybe he knew a secret God didn't want to share.

In the end, the absence of Henry and his miracle made the town hungrier for religion. People attended Sunday service with new vigor, and though Reverend Gregory initially met their enthusiasm with unease, he came to assume a confidence he'd never before possessed. There was something of Henry's determination now in the way he read the Gospels; when he looked up from the pulpit, his hands were sturdier, his gaze more controlled. Seasons passed, and after a year or two, nobody in Wyaconda brought up Henry Alexander's name.

But the specter of Henry was there: not just in the rapt attention of parishioners, and the new fortitude of the reverend, but in the way men at the bar spun long, fantastic stories to each other, evening after evening. And one summer night, while waiting for her husband to come home, Megan Pullman would find herself stopped cold by a vague sense of a time when she'd felt more loved, when someone spoke to her—clumsily but without embarrassment—wanting only to preserve her own invaluable soul.

ISABELLE AND COLLEEN

When I was thirteen I prayed for my brother and for his girlfriend, Colleen, because she was pregnant. I was sure that they had committed a terrible sin. I thought I was more scared than anyone; certainly, I was more scared than my brother. At thirteen, few things frightened me more than God and girls.

My mother and I had always gone to Mass on Sundays, but that year my father and Neil started going, too. My mother decided that attendance was no longer optional. Clearly, she said, this family needs the Lord. Nobody put up a fight. We were a quiet, sober bunch on those mornings before church. My father, brother, and I all wore collared shirts tucked into our pressed slacks. My mother had three dresses, and she rotated them throughout the month. We sat in the same pew each week, ten rows from the altar. My mother said she would have liked to sit closer, but this was as close to the priest as she could bring herself. When she said this, she was quick to remind us that pride is a serious sin.

In August I started the eighth grade. Neil and Colleen started their senior year of high school. Colleen was seven months big at this point. My family had known about the baby—and that Neil and Colleen planned to keep it—for four months. On the first Sunday after school started, my parents invited Colleen to Mass with us. She was Lutheran, and they knew she wouldn't come, but they invited her anyway, so that when she turned them down, they would have one more reason not to like her. The temperature was already in the low nineties that morning, and the air conditioner was broken at Our Lady of Pompano Beach. One of the old-lady volunteers had arranged stand-up fans in the aisles along the Stations of the Cross.

"Mother," I whispered, "God did not intend church to be this hot."

I was sitting between my parents, and we were listening to the homily. My mother did not turn her head. She was wearing her nicest dress, which was also the heaviest and thus—I assumed—the hottest.

I said, "I know you must be boiling in there."

My father said, "Jim."

"Aren't you hot, Dad?"

"Enough."

"I can barely concentrate in this heat." I couldn't stop myself once I got going.

"I'm not asking you to concentrate. I'm asking you to be quiet."

My mother looked at him. He had said the wrong thing. In a way, that's what I had been hoping for: that disappointed look.

Neil said, "It is pretty hot in here." He was sitting to the left of my mother.

"Both of you," my father said. "Enough."

I leaned back in the pew. I could feel the sweat between my back and undershirt. My skin had started breaking out the year before, and suddenly I was sensitive to things like pores. I took a look around the church. I kept a pious expression on my face and pretended to be in contemplation, but really I was looking for Isabelle. She was in my Algebra class, and I thought I might be in love with her. She was short with long black hair. She had breasts that pushed against her shirts. I didn't know if she would be at this Mass, but I knew she went to this church.

She had been in my CCD class a couple of years back when she came over from Cuba and could barely speak English.

"Look, it's happening again." My brother leaned over my mother to tap my knee. "It's bad this week."

I looked up at Father Riley, and sure enough, it was happening. His hands were shaking uncontrollably. He was trying to hide them, trying not to distract the whole parish with them, but it was impossible. When his hands got like this, he was incapable of even holding a Bible. Nobody knew why it happened. Father Riley wouldn't say.

I was worried about the devil, but the gossipy parishioners suspected booze.

"I hate seeing him like this." My father sounded almost angry.

"It only lasts a few minutes," I said, though this was not always true.

One of the old-lady volunteers hopped up from the first pew and turned the page Father Riley was reading from. Father Riley nodded, and the woman mouthed, "I'm sorry."

"Damn," Neil said.

"Say a prayer for Father," my mother said, turning toward each of us. "He prays for you."

There were changes in our house after Neil told us Colleen was pregnant. My mother took the news hardest. My father was angry—there was no doubt about that—but my mother seemed disappointed, as though she'd somehow let us all down. She drew up a list of ways to make the family closer. Along with going to church together, we started eating our meals together, including breakfast. Since my father had to be at IBM at 8:00, and my brother and I had to be at school at 7:30, breakfast happened early some days, before it was even light out. To make sure we were up, my mother woke first, getting breakfast ready for the rest of us. Not just cereal, either. Routinely, we had things like grapefruit, sausage, potatoes. We had to talk to each other while we ate. That was part of the deal.

When breakfast was ready, she called for us. Regardless of how dressed or awake we were, we sat at the kitchen table and ate as a family. On Monday morning my brother had coffee with his breakfast, which bothered my father. Neil had been drinking coffee since school started.

"Did you pour Neil his coffee yet?" my father asked.

"It's right there," my mother said, pointing to the table. She was finishing the eggs, but the rest of us were sitting.

"Good coffee," Neil said, taking a sip and rubbing his throat.

"Isn't it?" My father smiled. He looked as though he'd poisoned my brother and was waiting for the results.

"And the waffles: *magnifique!*"

I looked at my father and then at my brother. They were at opposite ends of the table, neither eating, each with a hand on his coffee mug. They shared the same thick arms and the same square-shouldered build. I sometimes wonder how it must have been for my mother to have a son so like her husband, and like him so soon.

My mother turned around, holding a skillet and spatula. She said, "You're not even eating."

"It's great," my father said, forking a piece of waffle into his mouth.

She looked at my brother. "Don't provoke your father."

Neil raised his hands in surrender. I drank my orange juice. As a rule, I stayed out of these things.

"We can have a nice breakfast." My father ate some more of his waffle. "We can talk about school. What are you studying right now, Jim? Some war? Is that right?"

This took me by surprise. "What do you mean, Dad?"

"Isn't that what you study: all the different wars?"

"In history class," my brother said.

"We don't have history."

"They have social studies," my mother said, pushing scrambled eggs onto each of our plates. "What are you studying in social studies, Jim?"

"Social studies?" my father laughed. "What is that, the politically correct version?"

"That doesn't make sense," Neil said.

My father dropped his fork onto his plate. It landed with a *clink* and bounced awkwardly onto the floor. It may have been an accident; I couldn't tell.

"I'll get you a new one," my mother said. "Just sit—"

"What doesn't make sense about that? That makes perfect sense to me." My father looked at me for approval. I nodded vaguely.

"Weren't we having a nice breakfast?" Neil said.

"We can have a nice breakfast," my mother repeated.

My father stood and grabbed a fork from the silverware drawer. He slammed the drawer shut, and my mother sat. "Does that make sense to you, Sarah?"

"It's not important."

"This one." My father pointed at Neil with his new fork. "He thinks he's an adult now, but he's got real responsibility coming his way." He held the fork in the air; it was at the same time menacing and ridiculous. "It's not going to be all cups of coffee and politics."

My brother held our father's gaze for a second before carrying his plate to the sink. "Come on," he said, picking up his backpack from the floor.

I picked up my backpack and brought my plate to the sink. I kissed my mother on the cheek. She told me not to let my brother drive too fast. My father kept his focus on his eggs.

The middle school was less than a mile from our house, and the high school was just up the street from the middle school. My brother and I had always walked to school together, but when Colleen got pregnant, my brother started driving. I still had to walk home after school, but I was happy for the morning ride. In August, the humidity makes walking anywhere in South Florida like walking into a wall of bricks. I was allowed to sit in the front until we got to Colleen's house.

What can I say about Colleen's house except that it was just about the nicest place I'd ever known a person to live in? I had seen plenty of big houses up and down A1A, but I'd never known any of the people who lived there. To me, those houses were landscape. Colleen's house was two stories and made of pink stucco. Her front lawn was bright green and full of trees that someone must have put there because I hadn't seen them anywhere else in Pompano Beach. Without fail, there was a shirtless man pruning something when we pulled up each morning. Colleen always spotted us from the window. We never had to honk the horn or go to the front door.

"How do you feel this morning?" my brother asked once we were on the road.

"Sore." Colleen answered the same way every morning. I didn't know where she was sore, which frightened me.

My brother put his right hand on her knee and steered with his left. "If you need it, you know where the medicine is."

The medicine was in the glove compartment. Some teenagers kept cigarettes in their glove compartment; my brother kept pain relievers for a pregnant woman.

"My parents were at it again last night. You know what they said this time?" Colleen didn't wait for my brother to answer. "They said they weren't ready to raise another child."

"They won't have to. You should have told them that," Neil said.

I always sat behind the driver's seat so I could watch Colleen. She had gained, I knew, sixteen pounds. Her weight was a constant topic of conversation on the ride to school. On this morning, though, she was distracted. She had each of her hands on her abdomen (I had learned to say *abdomen* and not *stomach*). Colleen's arms and face were still thin. Her beautiful brown hair was short and cut to what I assumed was the newest style. Her senior picture, it occurred to me, wouldn't look much different from her picture the year before. From a yearbook, nobody would know.

Colleen turned her head to look at me. Sometimes I was sure she knew I watched her. "How goes the eighth grade?" she asked.

"It goes."

"Big man on campus now."

"The biggest." Most of the girls were taller than me.

"Do you like it? Do you have your eye on anyone?"

My brother squeezed her knee. She looked at him and smiled. He tapped his left hand on the steering wheel and hummed the refrain to a song I didn't know. I didn't

like these personal questions. I didn't believe they were
interested in the answers.

"School is boring," I said. "There are lots of girls."
While not the whole truth, I decided that neither of these
two statements was false.

"Jim's a science whiz," my brother said. "He's going to
be a scientist."

At the time I did want to become a scientist.

"Answer me this," Colleen said. "How is it that there's
a human being living inside of me right now?" She turned
forward and laughed. "I mean, really?"

I didn't say anything. I expected my brother to make
some joke, or Colleen to keep talking, but neither of those
things happened. I put my backpack on my lap and stared
at it. I said six Hail Marys in my head, and then we arrived
at the middle school.

The eighth grade wasn't bad. My school went grades four
through eight, so I had plenty of opportunities to feel
superior. During lunch I sat at the table I wanted to. My
locker was tall and close to homeroom. At the end of the
year, we got to go to Cape Canaveral and be astronauts for
a day. Being an astronaut sounded like fun.

It was Algebra that I lived for, though. Algebra was fifty-
three minutes in the same room with Isabelle. I waited all day
for Algebra; it was seventh hour, the last period. Mr. Auletta,
a good-natured man with large glasses and shockingly hairy
arms, sat Isabelle in front of me. It was a decision based
entirely on the alphabet, but when I think back to the eighth
grade, I remember Mr. Auletta fondly for it.

After we got our first quiz back, Isabelle turned around to see how I'd done.

"Eighty-two." This seemed like a respectable score to me. I didn't want to tell her my actual score, which was ninety-seven.

Isabelle frowned and looked down at her quiz. "Did you get question three?" She sounded skeptical.

"X equals forty," I said, examining my own shielded quiz.

"I thought so! I thought so!" Isabelle raised her hand, and Mr. Auletta walked over. There were only two minutes of class left, and he had stopped teaching for the day. "I think there is a mistake on my quiz."

The prospect of a teacher's error drew the attention of the students talking around us. Shamelessly, they craned their heads toward Mr. Auletta while he quietly did the equation in his head. Finally, he nodded and changed the grade with a green pen.

"Sorry about that," he said before walking away.

The other students went back to their conversations, some with disappointed expressions. Isabelle's quiz now said ninety-seven percent.

"You got him," I said.

"What?"

"You caught his mistake. You got him."

Isabelle looked puzzled. "You didn't get an eighty-two."

I looked at my quiz. It was there for anyone to see, right-side up on my desk.

"Why would you lie about your quiz?"

I didn't know why. She made it sound like a very

foolish thing to do. I said what seemed most true, that I
didn't want to seem too smart.

Isabelle squinted at me. She had dark brown eyes
and thin dark eyebrows. I squinted back, and I saw a
laugh building behind her lips. We both leaned forward,
squinting. My heart was banging against my chest. What
I would have given right then to lean that much farther
and kiss her.

She said, "I don't get you, James." She was the only
person who called me James. I adored that word from her
mouth.

"What's there to get?" I said, feigning disinterest.

The bell rang, and everybody—Isabelle included—
hustled for the door. I stayed in my seat. I was the last
student to leave. Mr. Auletta walked over and asked me if
everything was all right. I told him that his class was my
favorite class.

My parents didn't go out to dinner much, but when they
did, Neil took note. My parents could be counted on to be
gone for no fewer than three hours, and as soon as they
were gone, he was gone, too, on his way to pick up Colleen.
I didn't know why Neil and Colleen liked sticking around
our house so much; all they did was watch television and
make popcorn. Maybe they liked the privacy. Maybe they
liked playing house. I sometimes wondered if Neil was
going to marry Colleen. I'd decided that if they came to
me with a plan to elope, I would help them escape.

I tried to stay out of their way when Colleen came over,
but that night they were sitting on the couch, watching

some old sitcom, and I was so bored I walked over and sat next to Neil. I didn't say anything, just pretended to enjoy the show, and when a commercial came, Neil slapped his palm on my shoulder and said, "How you doing, Brother Man?"

"I'm well." In an effort to sound more mature, I'd been saying *well* instead of *good*.

Colleen leaned forward and offered me the bowl of popcorn. She was wearing baggy pants and a loose top that revealed little of the contour of her body. She didn't look skinny but she didn't look seven months pregnant, either. I thanked her and took a handful of popcorn.

"We're watching *My Three Sons*," my brother said.

I nodded. I had never heard of this program.

"They don't make shows like this anymore." It was the kind of comment that would have annoyed my father.

"Do you like these shows?" I asked Colleen.

She shrugged her shoulders. It was clear enough to me that she didn't.

"These shows provide a historical record." Out of nowhere, Neil threw out phrases like *historical record*.

"You should study television history at college," I suggested.

Neil turned to me. "Here's what's great about them."

He pointed to the television screen, where the sitcom had resumed. Two men with slick hair were talking to each other in a backyard. Their clothes were tight, and the set looked cheap. I looked at my brother, and he was grinning widely. After a second, the laugh track came on, and he clapped his hands sharply. I couldn't understand any of it.

Then I thought about that title and Colleen sitting so quietly, and I asked her something I'd wanted to ask for a long time: "Do you know what the baby is?"

Neil answered. "We don't know. We chose not to know."

"What do you want?" I asked.

"I want a healthy baby," Colleen said. "We'll be happy with a boy or a girl."

"What if you have twins? What if you have three sons?"

"I don't have twins," she said.

This is what most amazed me: They were only four years older than I was.

I said, "I talked to a girl today." After all of these questions, I felt like I should volunteer something.

"You did?" Colleen leaned on my brother's shoulder. Her hair brushed against his cheek, and for a second I wanted to lean forward and touch it.

"I think she was flirting with me."

"I bet she was! Tell me."

When I finished my story, I realized what an awkward mess I had been. Neil looked a little embarrassed.

"That's flirting," he said, trying to sound encouraging.

"Absolutely." Colleen was ecstatic.

"I don't know what to do now," I said. "I guess I'll see her in school."

"You should call her," Neil said.

"Let's get the phonebook." Colleen rocked forward to get up, but my brother sprung off the couch and into the kitchen. He returned with the phonebook open in his right hand, as if he'd already found the number.

"What's her last name?" Neil asked.

"Hernandez."

He ran his finger down the page and whistled.

"She lives on Second Avenue."

Neil studied the phonebook and picked up the cordless phone. To my horror, he started dialing numbers.

"No, no, no."

"Here," he said, throwing me the phone.

"Hello," I said. "Hello?" The phone was still ringing. I hurried into my bedroom and locked the door. In the other room, I could hear Colleen chiding my brother.

A woman, energetic and not Isabelle, picked up. "*Diga.*"

"*Holà*, this is Jim calling—James from school—from Isabelle's class. I was wondering if Isabelle—I was hoping I could talk to her."

"*Isabelle?*" There was a long pause. I wondered if it was the wrong number. I threw myself onto the bed. I gripped the phone as hard as I could, half hoping it would snap and end my agony. "You speak to Isabelle?"

"I want to speak to Isabelle, yes."

"Hold on. Hold on."

I sat up and readied myself. I needed a plan: Why was I calling?

"This is Isabelle."

"This is James from school. From seventh hour. Mr. Auletta." I waited for some sound of recognition. When none came, I kept going. "I'm calling because I wanted to know if you had our homework assignment. I forgot it. I thought maybe you would have it."

"Did you want to copy mine?"

"I just wanted—"

"It's sort of late to be calling." I looked at the alarm clock beside my bed. When had it become 10:30?

"I just wanted to know what it was. So I could do it myself."

"The first ten problems at the end of Chapter Two."

"That's what I needed. So, thanks for that."

"James?"

"Yes."

"Do you like me?"

"Of course I like you."

Isabelle laughed. What did that mean? What had I admitted to? She said, "I like you too, James."

There was nothing to say after that besides goodbye. We hung up, and I exploded into the living room. But Neil and Colleen weren't there. I went to the window, and Neil's car was gone. The house was empty. I sat by the window, waiting for my brother to get back, so I could ask him what to do next.

Father Riley was incensed. The world, in his eyes, was a deeply flawed place. It was late Sunday Mass, and he was reading from Luke. He spoke sadly about dissipation and drunkenness. I didn't know what that word meant, *dissipation*, but I thought it sounded like everything melting into nothing. Just hearing it made me feel awful. When he lectured against alcohol, I saw people raise their eyebrows. Father Riley's hands were firm, though, and his voice was strong and severe. When he asked us to rise, my father stood with his arms at his side, his chin raised, as if he were taking orders from a drill sergeant.

At the end of Mass, my family filed out of the pew, quieter than usual, and made its way down the aisle. I was overwhelmed by my own wretched capacity for sin. I was uninterested in talking to anyone. When I felt a small hand on my forearm, I spun around, ready for attack. I was unprepared to find that the hand belonged to Isabelle.

"I saw you during Mass." She was wearing a plain white dress, and her dark eyes were looking up at me. I was short, but Isabelle really was small.

"Some Mass," I said cryptically.

"Some Mass," she agreed. We walked quietly. There were people all around us. "I just wanted to say hello. I should catch up to my family."

"You wouldn't want them to leave you."

"I'll see you in school, okay, James." Before she left, she touched my forearm again. I held my breath until I was outside.

For the past week in Algebra, Isabelle and I had hardly said a word to each other. There had been no mention of my phone call, of our mutual confession. She hadn't even turned around to see how I'd done on my quiz. I'd been convinced we were through. But now, this: two touches to the forearm. An unprovoked hello in a busy church. I felt my whole mood changing. There was hope for us yet.

During the ride back to the house, my father talked about Father Riley. In my father's opinion, Father Riley had really turned the corner this Mass. He'd taken charge, put us in our place. Wasn't that what a priest was supposed to do? My mother, who was driving, said that a priest was supposed to provide guidance. My father agreed, though they seemed to have different ideas about what guidance meant. I was still feeling good, but I could tell that something was bothering Neil. He was shifting around in his seat and pulling the seat belt off his chest. Occasionally, he would roll his window up and down for no good reason.

"We've got the air on," my father said.

"Dad," Neil said, looking right at him. "If I ask you something, will you promise to be straight with me?"

"Of course I will." My father looked at my mother and then out the window. He seemed confused. "Is this advice, a favor, what?"

"Something like that."

My father kept his eyes on the passenger side window. "So what is it?"

"I don't think I'm ready to ask yet."

I saw my father nod. He reached over and took my mother's hand, and for the rest of the ride they held hands, something I'd never seen them do before. I leaned over and asked my brother if he wanted to ask me his question, but he shook his head no.

Sometimes when dinner was over, and we were all sitting around the table with empty plates, my father would push back his chair and ask, Who wants a drink? My brother and I understood that we were exempt from this offer, so we would sit in our chairs and watch dumbly while my father poured my mother a weak gin and tonic. But that Sunday night my father looked at Neil when he asked his question. My brother seemed as shocked as I was. "Sure," he said, shrugging his shoulders, and like that my father came back with two Scotches on the rocks.

I could tell that my brother didn't know what to do with his drink. He stirred it with his finger, sipped from it, and smiled. He said, "This is good, Dad," as if my father had prepared it special, as if he hadn't just poured the thing out of a bottle.

I stayed in my seat. "Where's mine?" I asked.

"Enough of that, Jim," my mother said.

"Do you want one, too?" My father made it sound like a challenge. I thought about it. I didn't think I could keep down Scotch.

"I'll pass this time," I said. "I have school tomorrow." I thought it was a funny thing to say, but nobody laughed.

My mother said, "For God's sake."

"I was thinking," my father began, "that I haven't been completely fair with you, Neil."

My father took a long drink and looked into the glass. It was obvious he'd been preparing what he was going to say next. "You are an adult. You're almost eighteen, and you're going to be a father."

I got nervous. My parents didn't talk this way with Neil. They didn't use words like *father* in reference to him. I'd never once heard them say *baby*.

"All right. I know." My brother was talking quickly. "So what are you saying?"

My mother cleared the plates off the table. She started running the plates under water and placing them in the dishwasher. I got up to give her my glass, and when I handed it to her, she looked like she was about to cry. Her face was red, and her eyelashes were twitching. I didn't know what to do. I put my hand on her back and whispered, "Hey."

She gently pushed me away. "Go sit with your brother."

My father said, "Your mother talked to some people at the church."

Neil brought the glass to his mouth.

"Father Riley and the other one." My father looked at my mother for help.

"Father Luceri," she said.

"Father Luceri. They do work with an agency in Margate. A Catholic agency that helps people who have a lot on their hands." My father finished his Scotch and tapped his finger on the lip of the glass. "We were thinking, your mother and I, that maybe you could talk to them. Father Luceri gave us their number."

"What kind of agency?" my brother asked.

"A *Catholic* agency," my father said.

"What does the agency *do*, though? They do something, right?"

My mother wiped a dishtowel across her face and cleared her throat. "This is a lot, Neil," she said. "You know, it's a lot."

"What, Mom?"

"We just think you should consider it," my father said calmly. "That you and Colleen should talk to these people."

"Colleen and I know what we're doing." My brother was standing now.

"There are many, many people who would love to have

a healthy baby." My mother walked over to my father and put her hands on his shoulders. "Who could give the baby a home and attention. We talked to them, and they could have people ready."

Before my brother left the room, he looked at me. His jaw was clenched, and his shoulders were shaking. I shook my head sadly, but it could have meant anything.

My mother said, "I'm going to find him." When she got to the edge of the kitchen, she looked back at my father and said, as if to clarify, "I'm going to talk to him."

My father lifted his hand, and although I thought he was about to say something, he didn't, and my mother hurried off. It was a sad thing, watching my father sit there in silence, his hand still hanging in the air when it was just the two of us left. I wanted to reach out and take his hand—roughly but warmly in the way men sometimes do—and tell him, You didn't do anything wrong. What you said made sense.

But I didn't do that. I was thirteen, he was my father, and it didn't seem my place to tell him that I thought I understood what he was feeling.

"I was just twenty-three when we had Neil," my father said. "That was young. It felt young. But it wasn't seventeen."

"It was twenty-three." I wasn't trying to be a smart-ass; I was agreeing.

"Your mother was twenty-five. We hadn't even been married a year. He sounds like me. I mean, he sounds like me then."

"What do you think he's going to do, Dad?"

"Colleen has money. That will help."

"How will that help?"

"It just will. But I know. That's not what you were asking."

"Can you believe that Neil's going to be a father?"

"I think I can believe that. I do."

Neither of us said anything for a while, and when my father finally looked at me, I could see that he was as grateful for his lie as I was.

At 3:22 in the morning, Neil came into my bedroom, shut the door behind him, and sat at the end of my bed. He pulled my feet until I woke up, startled and swearing. This is what he told me later. I only remember the shock of seeing him. I remember him saying, "Watch your mouth, Brother Man."

"What are you doing?"

"I'm talking to you." I wondered if he was smiling. My eyes were adjusting to the dark, and I could barely see him.

"Why are you talking to me now? It's the middle of the night."

"I haven't been able to sleep. I've been up all night."

I pushed myself up against the headboard of my bed. I didn't think I could have a serious conversation lying down.

My brother said, "I want to talk about girls."

"I don't know much about that."

"How are things with your girl at school? What's her name?"

"I don't have a girl at school," I said. "But you mean Isabelle."

"You like her."

"Sometimes I think I'm in love with her."

My brother laughed. "That's great."

"Actually, it's terrible. We hardly talk."

"I know. You're not in love with her, though. You understand that."

I thought I understood that. "Why do you want to talk about girls?"

"I'm in a rough place."

"How's your girl?"

"She's going to have a baby pretty soon."

I could see my brother now, and I was surprised to find him fully dressed: jeans, sneakers, a collared shirt, undershirt.

"Are you going somewhere?" I asked.

"I'm going to Colleen's house."

"Are you eloping? I can help." I didn't entirely understand what it meant to elope, but I was confident it was a noble thing to do.

"I just need to talk to her."

"You can call her," I offered.

"I need to be with her." My brother stood and walked to my window. He peered through the blinds, as if expecting to see Colleen outside in our front yard. "Sometimes I'm jealous of you," he said. "Everything is still so innocent. You like a girl, and she likes you."

"It doesn't feel that easy."

"That's okay, though. I mean, that's right." Neil was pacing between the window and the bed now.

I crossed myself and whispered a prayer quiet enough that Neil couldn't hear me.

He looked at me. "What would you do?"

I felt my face grow hot. "I'm really sorry."

Neil walked to the side of my bed. He bent and pushed the tears off my cheek with his thumb. "I'll figure it out, Brother Man."

"I don't think you should go to Colleen's house," I choked.

"Why's that?"

"Mom and Dad will hear you leave."

My brother walked to the bedroom door. He was handsome in the dark, the shadows from the window sharpening his profile in black. Did he picture, I wondered, the baby growing up to look like him? How would my father react, seventeen years from now, to the prospect of another man carrying his heavy frame into adulthood?

"What were you going to ask Dad in the car?" I asked.

Neil put his hand on the doorknob. It was a simple gesture, but I had the sudden fear that without its support, he would collapse to the floor. "I was going to ask him if he could get me a job at IBM."

"But you're going to college."

Neil turned the doorknob and positioned himself in the open doorway. "I'm going to Colleen's house. If they wake up, cover for me."

"Tell Colleen I said hello."

As soon as Neil left the room, I jumped out of bed and went to the window. I pushed open the blinds and watched the driveway. I was full of fear and excitement in equal parts. I listened for the start of his car, and when I heard it, I adjusted my ears to listen for any movement within the house.

Neil was at breakfast the next morning. It was a sullen, serious breakfast without much talking, and I didn't think anyone but me noticed the red in his eyes or the almost frantic way he poured syrup and buttered his bread. We had pancakes and wheat toast, and Neil was out the door and into his car before I'd even put my plate in the sink. Before I left to join him, I looked at each of my parents, though neither revealed any knowledge of Neil's late-night trip. My parents seemed rested but worried, as though they felt guilty for the sleep they had enjoyed. When we picked up Colleen, I could see that she was just as tired as Neil. They didn't say anything the whole ride to school, and after they dropped me off, they turned left instead of right, which meant they wouldn't be going to school that morning.

For most of the day, I thought about my brother. I only participated when I had to in class, and in between classes, I wandered through the hallways absently until I stumbled through habit into my next classroom. What I was thinking was simple: What will my brother do? In my mind, it was entirely a question of what Neil would do. I liked Colleen, but she wasn't my brother, and I couldn't picture her deciding anything, even if the baby was growing inside of her body. But in Algebra I had a second thought: What if there is nothing to do? Colleen was going to have a baby, and Neil was going to be a father,

and they would have to find a way. It was my parents who
had created options: Keep the baby or don't. There were
no options for my brother, though. That decision had been
made a long time ago. The question—it occurred to me—
wasn't what will my brother do, but *how* will my brother
do?

I like to think that Isabelle could tell that all this
thinking had put me in bad shape. That her sensitivity
was the reason she turned around at the end of class and
talked to me with the kindest voice I'd ever heard from her.
I remember that when she turned around, she somehow
looked older. That it surprised me seeing her look older.

She asked, "Everything okay today, James?"

"Okay."

"You don't seem quite yourself."

"I think it's because I'm somewhere else."

"Do you know where you are?"

I thought about this question. "No," I finally said.

"I get that way."

Isabelle pushed her hair out of her face—a gesture
that typically sent my insides racing—and leaned forward
against the back of her chair. She brought her arms around
so that her hands were resting on the edge of my desk, and
I put my hands on the desk, too. We didn't hold hands,
or even touch, but from the surface of that desk, I felt a
sudden energy, a warmth up my arms and into my chest
that I had never felt before. Of course, I wasn't in love with
Isabelle. I was thirteen. But sitting in class, I felt for the
first time a feeling confused for love, a feeling that I have
felt more than once since and always called *love* before

I called it anything else. I don't know how to name that sensation, though I believe—as I recognized then—that there are few things more beautiful that move through the body.

"James," Isabelle said. We had been quiet for some time.

"Yes."

"We're just friends, right?"

"No," I said.

"We're not?" Her voice didn't sound surprised.

"We're together." The words were wrong, someone else's, and I knew it immediately.

She lifted her hands off my desk. "What do you mean, together?"

I felt like I had to do something desperate, that it was the only way to make things better. I slid out from my desk and knelt on the carpet beside her. I took my time doing this, thinking my brain would come up with something if I forced myself into the situation, but nothing came. I looked at Isabelle, and her eyes grew big. It must have seemed like I was proposing. The only other person to notice was Mr. Auletta. Without saying a word, he knelt beside the desk, too, assuming I'd lost a pen or contact lens and needed help finding it.

"I've got everything under control," I told him quickly.

"Four eyes are better than two," he said. "Six eyes, even." He laughed and pushed his glasses up the bridge of his nose.

Isabelle gave me a mournful half smile and turned to talk to the girl on her right. After a second, I pretended to find something, and holding my closed fist up as evidence, thanked Mr. Auletta for his help. He walked away contented, and I stared at Isabelle's long black hair, knowing she would stop turning around in Algebra, and I would not call her again.

There was no breeze on the walk back from school. My school was a good four miles from the shore, but in Pompano you'll sometimes get a kick off the ocean, still thick with salt, that carries over the roads and through the town, strong enough to mess up your hair. On that day, there was no such luck. The sun was heavy in the sky, pulsing in and out of focus and bending the blue around it. The sidewalk was littered with hairy coconuts and shriveled worms. I picked up a coconut and tried to crack it open, throwing it as hard as I could against the concrete, but it just bounced off and rolled into a yard. When I threw it again, it leapt right back at me, and threatened by this turn, I left it to roll into the street, where I was sure it would be crushed.

In my head, I played out the things I could have said to Isabelle. The things I could have done differently. On most days, the walk home took me twelve minutes, but on this day it took twenty. When I reached my front door, my chest and shoulders were dark with sweat. My hair was wet, and my face was slick. I only wanted to be inside the air-conditioned house. I wanted to take a cold drink into the living room, where I could watch television and quietly replay my humiliation.

The first thing I heard when I stepped inside was Colleen's laugh. I threw down my bag and walked into the living room. Colleen was on the couch, watching some dating show with what looked to be horribly mismatched couples. She turned her head to look at me and said, "I forgot you got home at this time."

"Is Neil here?" I hadn't noticed his car in the driveway.

"Nope. Just us. He went with your mom to pick out a graduation present for your cousin." Colleen looked at me. "It's going to be a pretty late present."

"No kidding." I had no idea what she was talking about. My parents didn't tell me about these things.

"They should be back in an hour." She motioned toward the television. "Sit with me."

I sat next to her, though I was still sweaty and thirsty.

"How is Isabelle?"

"She's well, but we're done." I mimicked an explosion with my hands.

"Oh no!"

"I sort of blew it."

"Is there any way to fix it?"

"Not that I can think of."

Colleen nodded knowingly. I realized that she didn't look tired, and it made me curious about where she and my brother had been all day.

"I know Neil went to your house last night," I said.

"He said you said hello."

"What did you do?"

"We talked. We were in my room. My parents' room is upstairs, on the other side of the house." Colleen stared forward, though she wasn't looking at the television. "My parents wouldn't have liked him being there at that hour."

"You didn't go to school today."

"We slept."

I wondered how Colleen slept. Could she sleep on her side? Did she have to sleep on her back? Did the baby sleep, too?

"*Ohhh.*" She placed her hands on her abdomen.

"What? What is it?" Images of Colleen going into labor, of me having to place my hands down there and deliver the baby myself, flashed through my head. "Are you all right?"

"I'm fine. The baby's just kicking. It surprised me a little."

"Does that hurt?"

"It's perfectly natural."

"I wouldn't want someone kicking me."

"It's not like that. Do you want to feel for yourself?"

I didn't want to put my hands on Colleen's belly. I was terrified that she was going to lift her blouse and make me put my hands on her actual skin. I looked to the front door, hoping somebody would come home.

"You don't have to," she said.

"Maybe I won't," I said.

Colleen leaned back into the couch. She picked up the remote control and turned off the television. "Can I tell you something?" she asked.

"Okay."

"I know what the baby is." She closed her eyes. I could tell that she hadn't told this to anyone else. I didn't know why she was telling me, but I was glad that she was. "It's a boy."

"How do you know?" I wondered if maybe a woman just knew these things.

"I could see from the sonogram. Then later I called the doctor, and she confirmed it."

"So it's official."

"Neil doesn't know."

I thought about that for a second. My brother and his girlfriend were going to have a boy.

"You're going to have a boy," I said.

"I *have* a boy," she corrected.

I watched her hands move slowly across her abdomen. "Is he still kicking?"

"He'll be kicking for the next fifteen minutes."

"Can I see?"

Colleen shifted slightly, so that her body was angled toward me. She took my hands and set them in the right place, over her blouse. I didn't feel anything and then suddenly I did.

"I can feel him kicking," I said. This surprised me. I focused my eyes on my own hands. My fingers would lift a little with each good kick. "That's your boy," I found myself repeating. "That's your boy."

Colleen nodded, and in my head, I wished him good luck. There were so many things we needed to learn, and I wanted to give him every secret I had.

PURITAN HOTEL, BOSTON

Cara couldn't believe her good luck. Five times she'd made this trip—from Boston to Montreal back to Boston—and not once, in either direction, had she been able to sit by herself. This time, the aisle was wet—all weekend it rained in Montreal—with dirt wedged into the rubber, but she wasn't put off, as she normally would be. The bus had pulled away with her red duffle bag planted firmly on the seat to her left, and there wouldn't be any big stops until she got off at South Station seven hours later.

She could sleep. Among the many things Cara could do without someone pushing into her space was sleep. Canada wasn't much to see—she would sleep through that—but she wanted to be awake for Vermont. Driving through Vermont in June was terrifying and beautiful. The highway wrapped around the side of the mountains, and in the tall bus, it always seemed as though the right-side wheels were spinning half on the road, half on air. The smallest bump or turn and they would be tumbling into the rivers and abandoned houses that filled the valleys and low hills beneath them. And the mountains were so green! That was what she first noticed, how uniformly and dazzlingly green they were, especially after the rain. *Ver-mont.* The Green Mountain State. It was true.

The bus reached a steady, smooth pace, and Cara looked out the window as Canada stretched flat before them. She liked making this trip by bus. It was cheap and it was relaxing. Every time she went to see her sister, she saw something new. There was the time she watched the bird's shadow—an eagle's? a hawk's?—darken over a bright blue river until the bird jerked its head beneath the water and came up with a fish in its beak. And there was the time she glimpsed the two children with no parents and colorful clothes walking along the edge of the highway in New Hampshire—laughing!—miles from a town in either direction. That had made her feel old. But she wasn't old. She was thirty-five then and thirty-eight now. Her sister Emily was already forty. Cara was the second youngest person in her office, including the secretaries.

Most of the seats were full. She really was lucky having the extra seat. She stretched her legs and smoothed her jeans with her hands. Who was on the bus? It was difficult to say. It seemed to be more travelers—she preferred the word to *tourists*—than business people. There weren't a lot of children, and she could understand that. Who would want to coop up their kids for seven hours on a bus? It wasn't like Montreal was built for children, anyhow, with the strip clubs and *artistes* asking for handouts. That was what killed her: eighteen-, nineteen-year-old men with healthy bodies asking for her money. She worked for a living. They could work, too. A handsome man, probably in his mid-twenties, sat diagonal from her in an aisle seat. He was reading a book that she imagined was serious by the way he held the pages and sat in his seat. Here was a man who had a job.

It made her want to read a book, but she'd already finished hers in Montreal. Her sister's house could be so boring at night. Emily went in before ten, and her husband, Pierre, was useless at conversation. It wasn't his fault. He hardly ever spoke English. The thing he was passionate about—separatism, predictably—he refused to discuss in English, which Cara thought was a little silly. The man diagonal from her leaned his chest forward and rolled his shoulders. He was thin, but his forearms were well defined. Cara coughed. She did it half to see if he would turn around, which he did. She smiled and touched her throat with her hand. He smiled back and said, "It's going around."

"Oh, it is," she agreed.

He turned back around, and why not? She sounded ridiculous. She sounded like she was seventy-five.

"Are you traveling on business?" Cara continued. Anything but, What are you reading?

He placed the open book—Henry Miller, of all things—on his thigh, spine up. "Visiting old buddies."

She introduced herself, leaning over her duffle bag to shake his hand. His name was Jack. *Jacques* in French, he said, with an obvious, too-loud laugh.

"I work in the city," Cara said. "In Boston, I mean. I was visiting my sister in Montreal."

"I can't say I much care for the place."

"Montreal? Why's that?"

"The filth," Jack said seriously. He drew a handkerchief from his pocket and wiped it across his forehead.

"I understand that Toronto is much cleaner." As if she knew such a thing.

They nodded at each other and then both looked down, Jack to his book, Cara to the magazine she'd slipped out of her duffle. She leaned against the window, content to read her magazine and snooze and watch the mountains for the rest of the trip.

The driver turned on the ceiling lights and slowed to a stop. Cara woke up startled, momentarily unsure of where she was. She felt for her duffle bag and pushed her glasses up her nose. She'd forgotten about the border checkpoint.

The driver—a woman, another first—stood and straightened her shirt in a deliberate, vaguely self-important way. She went through the drill: Everyone off the bus, bring your bags and suitcases, stay single file. Cara didn't have anything the authorities were likely to hassle her about. She wasn't entirely sure of the rules regarding international purchases, so she never brought back anything extravagant. This time: a jar of maple syrup and a bottle of merlot. The syrup was local, but the only

likely difference between the wine she'd bought and the
wine she might buy in Boston was the French label. She
was supposed to buy a carton of Gauloises for someone
she worked with, but Cara disapproved of her smoking—
the woman's teeth were a rotting row of yellow—and she
intended to pretend she'd forgotten.

Outside, in the hundred yards or so of borderland,
the weather was pleasant. Warm but not hot, the air thick
with water. It wasn't unlike, Cara thought, a bathroom five
minutes after someone has taken a shower. She held her
red Northwest Airlines duffle bag—a promotional gift—in
her right hand. She never brought more than the duffle; it
was a small point of pride. The line formed quickly without
her, and despite sitting close to the front of the bus, she
was somehow near the end of the line. The same fate had
befallen Jack, who one person in front of her possessed
nothing but a torn backpack. What did he keep in there?
A toothbrush, a few pairs of underwear, some crumpled
collared shirts, socks? Naturally, he had only the one
pair of jeans, which began to sag off his waist after days
without washing. More dirty classics? Lawrence, perhaps?
Baudelaire? Cara studied him. His shoulders were hardly
wider than her own. His hair had begun to curl boyishly
off the top of his neck. He was a pup. No more than
twenty-five. She could tell as much from his back.

"Ridiculous, isn't it?" Jack gestured at the line.

"Who's to say this bus isn't full of terrorists?" Cara
asked.

The man between them chuckled. He wore a full suit
and carried a brown briefcase.

"Does this take long?" Jack asked.

"It goes pretty quick. Most people, they don't even open the bags. Of course, if you're black, that's another story. Full body search." Why had she added that part? It wasn't true at all. "Some old maid will have forty pounds of ham, and there'll be a row. They'll let her keep it, but only after humiliating her for three minutes. One time a kid had cocaine or heroin—something—and they had to call in the Mounties."

"That sounds exciting."

She shrugged.

"What do you have?"

"Maple syrup."

Jack looked disappointed.

"And wine," she added.

"The syrup's excellent," the man in the suit interjected. "Better than the Vermont stuff."

Cara didn't want his endorsement.

The authorities—there were two of them—didn't open Jack's backpack. They didn't open the man in the suit's briefcase, either. When it was Cara's turn, they asked if they could look inside her duffle bag, their eager fingers already pinching the zipper. The young one seemed embarrassed when he brushed against her black bra, and the one with the fat face smiled when he held up the syrup, as though he and Cara were sharing a secret. Cara smiled back. "For my mother," she said.

The bus was surprisingly lively when Cara reboarded. The burst of fresh air and sense that everyone had gotten away with *something* had strangers suddenly chatty.

Jack, too. He was philosophizing the loss of baseball with a cheerful Québécois across the aisle. Jack was using his hands for emphasis, leaning out of the seat where her duffle had been.

"*Pardon*," Cara said, saying it the French way.

"Was someone sitting here?" Jack asked.

Cara tightened her grip on the duffle bag handles.

"I hope you don't mind my company," he continued. The Québécois grinned knowingly.

"I suppose not." She waited impatiently for Jack to get up so she could take the window seat.

She refused eye contact with the Québécois and tossed her duffle onto the floor by her feet.

Five minutes after they pulled away, the bus returned to its normal comfortable silence, punctuated with the occasional cough. Cara took out her magazine—a dignified version of the fashion, sex, and popular culture variety she'd been picking up since she was fifteen—and flipped past an article on menopause. How she hated the ubiquitous distinction between life before and after menopause, as though it were a precipice they were all crawling toward or gulf they were climbing out of. Jack was back to *Tropic of Cancer*, or *Tropic of Capricorn*, whichever zodiac he had reached. He was reading studiously, and Cara had to admit she rather liked having him here. He was younger, yes, but there weren't any worrisome maternal electrodes blinding her from the fact that he was, indeed, a good-looking man.

What would her sister think of this flirtation? Could you even call it that? Cara knew what Emily would think. She would think it absurd, though she'd deliver her support in a buoyant, overexcited way. That was her thing: Emily was always being *supportive*. Supportive of Cara's ill-conceived idea to restore the apartment in Cambridge, supportive of their mother's halfhearted yoga, supportive of Pierre's clandestine poetry writing. Cara laughed when Emily showed her some of the secret verse—Cara could read French better than speak it—and the look of hurt on Emily's face convinced her instantaneously that it was one of the cruelest things she'd ever done. But why couldn't Emily just be honest? Why couldn't she say the apartment's a wreck, I give the yoga two weeks, Pierre, dear heart, your poetry is dreadful. *Terrible.* Were Emily here right now, sitting where Jack was sitting, why couldn't she be straight with Cara: Spare yourself the embarrassment.

Jack placed his hand on her thigh. It rested there softly, thoughtlessly, like a sparrow on a tree branch.

"May I read you part of this?" He pressed gently.

"We'll take turns. You read me your smut, and I'll read you mine."

Jack read Cara a short passage. It wasn't dirty, or overtly flirtatious. Cara thought she might have liked it had she not been concentrating on keeping her leg still and her hands folded over her lap.

"It's very nice," Cara said.

"I think so."

"I'm not going to read you part of my magazine."

"That's fine."

"Well, maybe I will."

"Whatever you want."

His hand was so light on her thigh—no heavier than

a book or an iPod—and still she could feel the individual
weight of each of his fingers, the casual heaviness of
his thumb. Her own hands were warm, her long fingers
jammed together. Certainly, *this* was noteworthy. Then, a
frightening thought shuddered through her: What if he
wanted something? To be sure, she didn't have much on
her. Just the red duffle bag. But there was her wallet. All
the credit cards, fifty or sixty dollars cash, a purse full of
coins. These were unfair thoughts, though. Unfair to Jack,
unfair to herself. Why shouldn't he want to talk to her?
She was interesting, funny, reasonably attractive. It was a
long bus ride. Henry Miller only got you so far.

"I'll give you a choice," Cara said. "Tips on shaving
your legs or easy ways to add fiber to your diet."

"What good is fiber to me?"

"What good are shaved legs?"

He blushed and withdrew his hand. So Jack could
be embarrassed. It only made sense that he could be
embarrassed, yet something about the rush of blood to his
cheeks—that generous stroke of red—pleased her. He was
most handsome when he blushed. His vulnerability was
reassuring.

"If it makes you feel any better, I wax my legs," Cara
lied.

"Now I know more about you than you know about
me."

"Well."

"I'm a spy. I'm the Canadian James Bond."

She surveyed him quickly with her eyes. "No," she said
definitively.

"Obviously, there are going to be differences."

"I don't see any way you could be a spy."

"Ergo, my effectiveness."

"I would need evidence."

He put his lips to her ear. He whispered some nonsense—international intrigue, everyone out to get him, who could he trust?—and it was words, but mostly it was those two lips fluttering like butterfly wings. She looked out the window while he whispered, watched the light rain that had started again and didn't seem to fall so much as scatter. She thought about meteorology, the clichéd idea that the flapping of a butterfly's wings could cause, through chaotic escalations within the atmosphere, a disturbance as large and unpredictable as a hurricane.

They talked through Vermont. Cara was unable to appreciate the mountains because they talked so much. Into New Hampshire they talked, and New Hampshire felt short—she knew the state only as a bridge between other places—so they talked into Massachusetts, as well. By then, it was dark. She turned on the reading light above her so she could see his face.

It was not, Cara had come to realize, a distinctive face. Handsome, to be sure, but somehow ordinary. There were no dominant features—long nose, high cheekbones, dark eyes—but rather a general, unblemished attractiveness. His hair was cut short, and he had little ears. The most identifiable aspect of his countenance may well have been his surprisingly small ears. When he smiled, and he did often, it was in the trained way; he only smiled naturally when he laughed, which happened less frequently.

Jack was from Ontario, so they talked about that. It turned out that he disliked French Canada, or more accurately most French Canadians, but he assured her this sentiment was not atypical among Canadians. Cara offered that she disliked Southerners, not because it was true, but to be polite. They talked about Emily and about Jack's brother Jason—yes, they all had names that began with *J*, he didn't know why his parents had done it—and about the weather. There were pauses when they didn't talk, but they were filled with reading, or appreciative nodding, and there was only a little awkwardness. To stress a point on one occasion, Jack placed his hand on Cara's forearm. On another occasion, to show that she thought his story was funny, Cara tapped his knee.

They talked into Boston, which appeared out of the darkness as a string of lights that arched upward.

"Where do your friends live?" Cara asked, her eyes half-fixed on the city's outline.

Jack looked puzzled.

"The *old buddies* you're here to visit."

"Right."

"Because I probably know the neighborhood. Just me being curious."

"About that." Jack took out his handkerchief and wrapped it around his hand. "I made up all that."

Cara felt a slight pang of panic.

"I'm interviewing. I said the thing about visiting friends because I didn't want to get into it."

"Into what?"

"Well." Jack sighed, as though a great burden had been lifted from him. "When I tell people I work for the airlines, they always ask why I take the bus."

"Why do you?"

Jack laughed, flashed the natural smile. "The things I see, you know? It's like working at a restaurant and being inside the kitchen. I don't work with buses—"

"Where are you interviewing?" Cara interrupted.

"Northwest. They're the best of the lot."

"So you're staying at a hotel."

"Any recommendations?"

Cara had the sense that she was being lied to, but what a strange lie. Why hadn't this come up earlier? "I don't know the hotels so well."

"There's a hotel in Beacon Hill I heard about. Do you know Beacon Hill?"

Cara knew Beacon Hill. She'd always wanted to live there, so close to the Statehouse and the Common and with all those narrow, regal apartments. It was how she pictured London, which she'd never been to, though she'd been told she would love it. Beacon Hill is expensive, though. Why take the bus to stay at an expensive hotel?

"It's pricey," Cara said. "You might be better off with one of the Puritan Hotels."

Jack nodded to suggest that this option had occurred to him.

The bus slowed in the traffic of the city, and people began to stir, zipping their bags, gathering their belongings, plotting a quick exit. The Québécois across from them rubbed cologne on his neck and brushed his shirtsleeves compulsively, as if to scrape off the communal smell of the bus. The driver announced South Station, and Cara remembered that the bus always pulled into the stop quicker than she expected. She looked at Jack, who was stuffing his book into his backpack. She was sad— ridiculous as it was—at the prospect of never seeing him again. Now that she'd gone to see Emily, she wouldn't see her again until Thanksgiving. She saw her parents plenty, and that was fine, and of course there were the people she worked with. But wasn't this different?

"Are you going straight to your hotel?" Cara asked.

"I figured that would be best."

"Maybe we could get a drink." She was never this forward. It was exhilarating to hear her own voice. "There's probably a bar at your hotel. We could go over together."

"I think I will stay at one of those Puritan Hotels."

Cara nodded.

"A drink sounds good," Jack said.

Cara hadn't been thinking. There wasn't a bar at the Puritan Hotel. She should have known as much.

"It looks like we're in trouble," Jack said, looking around the lobby.

"Want to grab two forties?" Cara asked. "I saw a packie on the way over."

Jack frowned.

"We can drink them on a park bench. Pretend we're delinquents. It'll be fun."

"What's a *forty*?"

"Oh, right. You guys are on the metric system."

"What's a *packie?*"

The woman at the check-in desk shuffled papers noisily. She didn't seem to understand why a man and woman would be in a hotel lobby and not paying for a room.

"I'm sure there's a bar nearby." Cara could feel the night slipping away from her. "A few blocks in either direction—"

"It's getting late." Jack looked at his wrist. He wasn't wearing a watch. "I think we should just stay."

"We could stay."

"If we stay, we can use the mini-bar."

Cara didn't object, though she was almost certain that there weren't mini-bars at the Puritan Hotel.

"All right. Well, if you'll excuse me." Jack headed toward the men's room.

"Excused," Cara said, suddenly feeling old, suddenly feeling like she was his teacher, and this was all a cruel joke.

There were only a few seconds of silence before the woman at the check-in desk called Cara over. "So, you want a room," the woman said, pushing a pen and check-in form across the counter. "You want a single or a double? Here are the prices."

"Oh, I was going to wait."

"Listen." Her name tag said Suzanne. Her breath smelled of mint, and her left eye moved on its own. "Let's not play games."

"I'm not playing games." Cara was insulted. She wanted to defend herself, to call this woman *Suzanne* in an indignant way, but Cara was nervous, and that would be rude, and she didn't want to be the sort of person who read name tags indignantly.

"You're not playing games. But this room isn't paying for itself. Wonder boy there isn't going to pay, is he? So you're going to pay. It's a hundred dollars for a single."

Cara opened her mouth, but she didn't know what to say. She signed the sheet. She reached into her duffle bag and gave Suzanne her Visa card.

Jack stepped out of the men's room still rubbing his hands dry.

"I got a room," Cara said.

"Why in the world did you do that?"

"You needed a room."

"Let me pay you for it." Jack pulled out a roll of bills and handed her five twenties. She hadn't expected him to give her anything, for him to have money at all. Something about the exchange felt cheap, but she liked that he wanted to pay, that he hadn't asked before reaching for the bills.

"Thank you," Cara said, putting the money in her wallet and lifting her bag onto the check-in counter so she could place her wallet inside.

The credit card machine pushed out a receipt, and Suzanne tore it off and gave it to Cara. Suzanne handed the key card to Jack and nodded at the elevator. "506," she said brightly.

Jack placed his hand on Cara's back, and they walked toward the elevator. It was comforting having that hand on her back. There were two elevators and a flight of stairs. Cara guessed the left elevator would come first, and Jack guessed the right. It was childish—silly, really—but Emily

would have to agree that certainly *this* was something.
Emily would have to concede that going to a man's hotel
room—having that man's hand on your back while you
both teetered back and forth, laughing over which door
would open first—meant *something*. The whole ride over
on the subway Cara had wondered if people thought
she and Jack were together. They sat together and talked,
nothing unusual, but the looks they exchanged suggested
a certain intimacy. Didn't they? Were she somehow
watching them from the other side of the subway, wouldn't
she think: Those two are together? The left door opened,
and Jack took his hand off her back. She wouldn't tell
Emily everything later. She would be selective with her
information. Being selective would make the whole thing
that much more appealing.

The hotel room was plain and unadorned. There was a
wide bed along one wall and a large window opposite the
door. The curtains were pulled shut, and the lights were
off. Jack threw his backpack onto the bed and flipped on a
light switch. When the door closed behind them, it locked
loudly.

Cara dropped her duffle bag and walked to the bureau.
"No mini-bar," she said.

Jack didn't say anything. In the mirror above the
bureau, Cara watched him rummaging through his
backpack.

"I thought there might not be one," she continued.

"It's fine."

"We could open that bottle of wine I bought."

"We could do that."

"I think I'll open that bottle."

Cara knelt beside her bag. She looked up when she found the bottle. Jack was standing there with a small black handgun.

Cara had never seen a gun before. Not in person. She was surprised at how simple it looked. It seemed a very singular thing: There was one color and one trigger, one handle and one hole. She could examine the gun closely because it was no more than two feet from her face. Jack held it away from him, as though he were scared it might go off of its own volition. Cara thought about how much it looked like a toy gun. Perhaps, she reasoned, it really was a toy gun. Cara tightened her grip on the wine bottle. She lowered her eyes and said what she thought he wanted to hear: "My wallet is in the bag."

"I know where your wallet is."

"All right."

"Keep your eyes down." Jack didn't sound that different. He sounded slightly strained, the way a person might sound if he were trying to find his car keys in the morning.

"You're not going to shoot me."

"Of course I'm not going to shoot you." Jack stepped forward and kicked the duffle bag away from her. "Do you know how stupid it would be if I shot you?"

Cara didn't say anything.

"It would be very stupid. But I will shoot you if you move."

"I won't move."

"I know you won't."

She looked at her hands. They were wrapped tight

around the neck of the bottle, and still they shook badly. She didn't want to die here. Jesus, what a place to die. She didn't have much, and he would be disappointed, but hopefully he would just go. Her knuckles were frighteningly white.

"If you do anything with that wine bottle, I'll shoot you," Jack said.

She dropped the bottle. It rolled to the foot of the bed.

"I have your wallet."

"All right."

"Look at me. I have your wallet and now I'm leaving. I didn't take anything else."

Cara raised her head, though it pained her to do so. She was scared that when she looked at him, he would shoot her. Jack was standing above her with his backpack on. He wasn't holding the gun anymore and he wasn't holding the wallet. He was packed and ready to leave. Cara couldn't help it: She started to cry. She was holding all the noise inside, and it was just tears. She could feel them pushing down her cheeks and see them falling off her face. Jack pulled the handkerchief from his pocket and wiped her face with it.

"I'm sorry I have to do this," he said.

"You don't have to." She was surprised at the words.

"No, I have to. It's complicated, but I have to."

"I don't understand."

"There's nothing to understand." Jack glanced quickly at the door.

"You need money. You're in debt or on drugs. You have a girlfriend who's in trouble."

"Money. Sure. Of course it's money." Jack took a heavy step forward and then pointed to the window at the back of the room. "What you need to do is stand against that window."

Cara couldn't stand. She wanted to—she wanted to do everything he said, for this to be over—but she couldn't make herself.

"I can't," she said.

"What do you mean you can't?"

"I just—I can't."

Jack extended his hand—the same hand he'd held the gun in, the same hand he'd wiped her face with—and she took it. His grip was strong. His palm was slick with sweat. He pulled her up, and when she was standing, she looked at him. He looked at her, and his expression told her nothing. It had been foolish to trust him, and now she was being robbed. He pushed her gently in the direction of the window, and she found, to her relief, that her legs would take her there.

"I want you to stay along that window." Jack was quiet for a moment. "Don't make any noise."

"I won't."

"Don't talk to anybody."

Cara shook her head.

Jack walked backward to the door. He opened it quickly and left. Cara listened to his feet pounding down the hallway until the door closed, and then the room became quiet.

Cara counted to sixty before she moved. She took even steps to the door and locked the deadbolt. She turned around anxiously, as if he might still be in the room, but there was only the thin mechanical hum of the air conditioner. She walked to the bed and tore off the comforter, as if it were concealing him. Cara tore off the blanket and the hard white sheets. Digging her fingers beneath the mattress, she pulled off the bottommost sheet, so that the bed was bare. Then she sat on it and buried her feet in the sheets and blankets heaped on the floor. She thought to herself: You are safe. What is important is that you are safe.

But Cara couldn't stop thinking about how stupid she'd been. How needlessly she'd jeopardized her safety by trusting a stranger. Was there any rule more apparent than the one that warned against following strangers? There were plenty of women, she knew, who did this very thing, who followed strangers back to their hotel rooms, but she wasn't one of those women. That was where she had gone wrong. She pretended to be someone she wasn't. She was suffering for that indiscretion now. It didn't seem unfair.

Except that it did. It felt very unfair, and Cara allowed self-pity to overwhelm her, if only for a second.

She picked up her phone. Reporting what had happened was the responsible thing to do. She dialed Emily's phone number.

"*Allô.*" It was Pierre.

"Is Emily there? It's Cara."

"*Naturellement.*"

Cara opened the curtains, and the view surprised her. She could see more of the city than she'd expected. The streets beneath her were lit and sprinkled with people.

The new downtown building stood unshy in the distance, shorter than the buildings around it but better dressed. From this window, Boston was younger than the city she lived in.

"Are you in?" Emily asked. "When did you get in? It's late."

"I was robbed," Cara said. "My wallet."

"You were robbed? What a thing to have happen."

"It happened at the bus station."

"Cara, are you all right?"

"I'm fine. The whole thing—it was disorienting, you know?"

"Are you still there?"

"I'm home now." The lies came to Cara easily. They came without thought and with the understanding that they would not be taken back.

"What are you going to do? Your driver's license, your credit cards."

"He has it all," Cara agreed.

"He knows where you live."

Cara wasn't prepared for Emily's pragmatism. Everything Emily said—obvious as it was—occurred to Cara only when she heard it.

"I need to change my locks."

"He doesn't have your keys, does he?"

"No, I suppose he doesn't."

"You're frightened," Emily said. "I wish I were there."

Cara leaned against the window and looked around the room. Here was the bureau, and her duffle bag, and the wine bottle at the foot of the bed. How could she ever tell

Emily this? The duffle was zipped shut. Jack had closed it when he was done with it. Probably, Cara thought, zipping the bag seemed the natural thing to do.

"I'm tired," Cara said, though this was not true.

"I really do wish I were there."

"I need, I think, to go to bed."

"You'll call me," Emily urged. "When you feel better, you'll call me."

Cara hung up. She looked out the window again, at the people walking in different directions. She looked for Jack but, of course, she didn't find him. For the rest of her life, Cara knew, this would be a story she would tell. The time that she was robbed. She would alter the facts, depending on the listener—never revealing to anyone the whole, sordid truth—and attach to those facts a gamut of emotions: fear, helplessness, outrage. She would alter the facts but she would never forget what actually happened. What Cara would forget is that talking to her sister, Cara didn't feel any of those things. That for a time she only felt lonely: a loneliness so physical it was a part of her, a second tongue that shaped her every word, a muscle so strong and necessary she was certain it had always been there.

ON THE HIGHWAY NEAR FAIRFIELD, CONNECTICUT

It was a phrase we both used. We liked the ring of it, I suppose. It was a convenient phrase and it came in handy. Anytime anyone asked what religion I was—often worded simply as *what* I was—I answered the same way. And my cousin Carolyn answered the same way, too. Lapsed Catholic.

The phrase wasn't unique, picked up from an aunt, or maybe overheard in a conversation. Lots of people used it. But that's no matter. My cousin and I treated the phrase as our own. It came up as we were pulling through the dry rust of New York into bluer Connecticut.

"Because you can't be a lapsed Presbyterian, or Lutheran, or Baptist," Carolyn said, looking at me from behind the steering wheel. "A lapsed Baptist. That just sounds ridiculous."

"A lapsed Southern Baptist," I added.

"Ridiculous."

"So how can you be a lapsed Catholic?"

"I don't know, Daniel. You just can."

"That's true," I said.

We were on our way to Cape Cod for Easter. Carolyn worked in D.C., and I worked in Baltimore. We decided it would be easier if we took one car to see our family. Neither one of us had much money, though she had a little more. She's also a little older, though I'm smarter. That's a hell of a thing to say, I know, but it's true. She's more attractive. I'll give her that.

We've always been pretty close. For no good reason beyond familiarity, really. We grew up together. Took baths together, scraped knees together, snuck drinks together. She's a good person. We're both lapsed Catholics. It kills our parents to hear us say it. Her mother's the best. Puts her hands over her ears and says, I'm not hearing this, Carolyn, I'm not hearing my only daughter singing with the devil. My mother's not nearly as fun. She just gets red and sad and brings up a favorite phrase of her own. Jesus, Mary, and Joseph. Or sometimes Holy Mary, Mother of God.

"I'm not saying we're better or anything," Carolyn said.

"We?" I asked.

"Well, we're *culturally* Catholic."

"Right."

We were going eighty-five miles per hour in Carolyn's Honda. The windows were halfway down, and Carolyn's hair kept getting wrapped around her sunglasses. She had long blond hair. Sometimes her hair was red. Originally, it was brown. For Easter it was a stylish blond. Festive but respectful. She was wearing jeans and a sweatshirt, though it was understood she'd change into something nice for Good Friday.

"You know, everyone smokes cigarettes," Carolyn said.

"Everyone?"

"Not everyone, but all adults. They sneak them. It's a big secret."

"Like Uncle Richard," I offered.

"Exactly like Uncle Richard."

Mostly, Carolyn kept the car in the far left lane. Sometimes she passed cars on the right. She slowed a little when she went up hills. She noted the different restaurant logos on the large rectangular signs off the highway.

"Wendy's. Do you like their hamburgers better?"

"No," I said. "They always sort of taste like eggs to me."

"I do."

There was no music playing. Carolyn wouldn't allow it. She said that people should talk in cars, that people don't need music. Some of the best conversations she'd ever had were in cars, Carolyn explained, and there was never music playing when they happened.

"We should talk," I said.

"Sure."

"How's work been?"

"Fine. Busy."

"How's Allan?"

"He's good. A little fatter."

"Really." It seemed like a funny thing to say. "How much fatter?"

"Quite a bit," she said.

Then it was the part of the highway where the ocean creeps up from behind the pine trees and stretches out along the road. In Fairfield, Connecticut, the ocean is a flat, disinterested blue.

"I always forget you can see water here," I said.

"Allan's been difficult lately," Carolyn said.

"Difficult?"

"We don't talk. Not at all."

We passed a harbor with clean docks and still flags.

"You like to talk," I said.

"I know, Daniel."

"I don't mean that in a bad way."

"You do, but that's all right."

"Have you talked to Allan about this?"

"What's there to say?" she asked. "He's bored with me. I bore him."

"You don't know that."

"How's Shannon? I like her."

I'd met Shannon two years before in Baltimore, my first year out of college, when I had a part-time job with an ill-tempered history professor at Goucher. The professor was trying to put all this information—I say information because I never really found out what he was researching—on the internet. The department was pressuring him to do it. Throwing lots of money at him. But the professor was old and tenured and didn't have any real interest in putting anything on the internet. So I did a little paperwork, and he reorganized the project each week. There were a series of false starts, as he called them. Shannon was one of his students. I got to know her after she stopped by his office.

"Shannon's doing well," I said. "She graduates in a month."

"What's she studying again?"

"Economics."

"So she'll be making the money," Carolyn said.

"I guess you could say that."

"Would you say that?"

"I guess."

Shannon isn't Irish but she has an Irish name, and that had been enough for my family when she came to visit. What do you mean is she Irish, I heard my mother say to my grandmother in the kitchen. Her name's Shannon. Do you need her to do a jig on the living room table?

"Shannon's very attractive," Carolyn said. "She has those eyes. You can have boring brown eyes and you can have beautiful brown eyes, and hers are beautiful."

"I know."

"She should do something with her hair, though."

"Her hair is sort of long."

"She'd look better with shorter hair. More professional."

The speedometer bounced to ninety. I was keeping an eye on it. I never drove this fast on my own. Except for the first day. The day I received my driver's license, I pushed my mother's Buick to a hundred, then took my foot off the pedal and coasted. It was near midnight when the highway was empty. As a teenager, on my own, it seemed important to go a hundred miles per hour.

"You love Shannon, right?" Carolyn asked.

"Yes."

"I don't know if I love Allan anymore. It's hard to tell sometimes, you know?"

"It is."

"You don't know. You're in love. You don't know anything when you're in love."

"You know some things," I said.

"No, you don't know shit," she said, staring at me with her chin crunched up and white. "It's the greatest thing in the world."

"Carolyn," I said.

"What?"

"Carolyn—"

When I was sixteen, I worked with my Uncle Richard at an auto shop in Harwich. I learned, among other things, that the brake system of cars is twofold: There is a foot brake and a hand brake, and the hand brake is the emergency brake. The emergency brake, I knew, was what you used when you were parking on a steep incline or coming upon a yellow light too quickly. It was what you used, as I later found, when you were driving ninety miles per hour on the highway, and your cousin said your name, said it twice, because there was a car in front of you, and you were going to hit it. The emergency brake was what you used when you engaged the foot brake, but the foot brake froze (too much pressure for the hydraulic pump), and you didn't know what to do, how not to kill your cousin, the way not to die. I knew, from sulking around the shop while my uncle heaved over engines, that the emergency brake affected the rear wheels only. That the front wheels kept moving. That they were as unaware of what was happening as your body, which was only your body, and not you. You were somewhere else, sheltered from the sudden physics of it all.

That, I knew, was a gift.

Everything else, I did not know. How, for instance, time slows. How time, as if removing a watch face, or opening a man's chest, quiets to show you how things work. How when time slows, you see that the subtle movements of the universe are not beautiful, as you always suspected, but awkward. How surprising that is.

When you have time, you see that human faces are forever moving and that smiles are easily forgotten in the mechanics of blinking. You realize that sound is always detached from sense in the way that thunder follows lightning. You find that tastes, to your frustration, do not leave your mouth. When time slows, you understand that there is no time to panic because there is too much time for reaction to function. So instead of reacting, instead of saying your cousin's name for a third time, you think, I am still here. There are green veins thick across my hands. My breaths are long and uninflected. You do not think, as you may have thought, We're going to hit that car. Or, perhaps, This wasn't my fault. You do not think, as the car slides into the middle lane and then the right lane, of any of the things you expected to think about before dying.

Here is what happened. Carolyn slammed the brakes

then pulled the emergency brake and finally turned the wheel hard to the right. All of that happened in one second, or so it seemed: Those actions were the last in normal time. After that I expected my life to flash before my eyes—that was supposed to come next—but instead I saw something different.

What I saw, with perfect clarity, was Shannon on the first night she came to my apartment. She was wearing an amber blouse and black shoes and a knee-length black skirt. Her hair was folded into a tight, brown knot. She wasn't wearing makeup—she never does—but she was wearing just enough lipstick to make you wonder if she was wearing lipstick, and that seemed right. All her movements, I understood as I watched them again, were calculated. The way she crossed her legs and gently ironed her skirt with her hands when sitting. How long she lifted her eyebrows and looked at me when I offered her a drink. She refused the drink, and that was calculated, too. I made myself a highball and put a glass of water on the table in front of her. We sat on the couch and didn't say anything for whole seconds until I asked her if she liked jazz, and she nodded. I got up and put on the only jazz album I owned. The trumpet came in on the first track in a sad, desperate sort of way, and it made us both nervous. Shannon asked me if I liked jazz, and I said that I was just getting into it. It was ten o'clock, and we didn't have any plans for the night.

Shannon put her hand on the library book lying on the table and asked if she could look at it. She placed the book square across her lap, and I came closer and explained that I'd checked it out because I was going to see the Van Gogh exhibit at the National Gallery, and that I didn't know much about his work. She told me she'd only seen his paintings on posters in dorm rooms. The sunflowers, the purple room with the crooked bed. Everyone likes the starry night, she said, but I don't care for it as much. She told me she'd seen one with sailboats that looked like they were tied to the edge of the painting, and it was her favorite. We looked for the painting in the book and when we found it, she smiled and said, Yes, that it *was* the best one she'd ever seen.

I told her about the painting I'd been looking at. That it was the only one I'd really been looking at. I told her that it was going to be at the National Gallery. That my friend had said it was the last painting in the exhibit, and that it was appropriate because it was the last one Van Gogh ever finished. Real long, my friend said of the painting, and bigger than you'd expect. It looked, he said, heavy. We were sitting closer now, and I placed my right hand on her back. She flipped to the end of the book, figuring the painting, if it was his last, must be the final burst of color before the columned regularity of endnotes and the index. It was. She ran her hands across its glossy surface. I feel like I should be able to feel the thickness of it, she said, staring at her own fingers. They should make them so you can feel the paint strokes.

We looked at the painting for a while, not saying much, just looking. Shannon began tracing her finger along the road in the middle. When her finger reached the horizon, she picked it off the page and asked, Why do you like this one? It's the pictures, I said without really thinking, my right hand stretching in the air behind her back. They're inside the painting, I explained. Faces and shapes. Bending, breaking. They're everywhere. She touched her neck. I can show them to you, I said. They're in the strokes. He put them there.

Shannon brought the book near her face, and I couldn't see her face, so I thought about what the painting looked like. I said to her, There's a lot of yellow in the painting. There's a lot of blue, too, but there's so much yellow. There are no trees to break it up. Only wheat. There are crows, · flying out of the black, carrying the black with them, leaving the night blue. They're making space for a moon, I told her, but it might be a sun, or it might be both. There'd be more black in the night if it weren't for the crows. Or more blue if it weren't for the night. Shannon held the book in front of her face. The red and green don't really change anything, I continued. It's just yellow wheat and black crows. I paused, thinking about what Shannon looked like behind the book. But the pictures are in yellow, I said. That's all I meant to say. That they're there.

Shannon steered the book back and forth, adjusting her vision. She asked, How do I find them. Look closely, I said. Forget it's a painting and just think of the colors. Or the strokes. Follow the movements. You'll forget it's a painting. You'll forget I'm even here. She lowered the book and smiled and then raised the book. It was the last time I saw her face. Not ever. Not the day it happened. But the day I was seeing it all again. It was the last time I saw her that day. Because the car was slowing—the wheels gaining traction, the engine cooling—and we weren't going to die. We were going to stay alive, and there wasn't going to be any more time.

But I needed more time. Time for the shapes to twist out of the strokes. Time for the faces to say something, or nothing, in yellow or blue. Time for Shannon to see it happen. Because she did. When she saw the pictures, she made a sound, neither voice nor breath, but merely a manipulation of air through lips and teeth. Time knew this. Heard the sound. Saw how the oxygen shrank. Felt the slight change in temperature that accompanied it. Time feels most intensely the currents that navigate endlessly through and around the things that make up the world. Time knows too well that before there was time, before there was anything, there was air, nameless and contained in a pocket darker than any hole in history, and only the size of a human fist.

Time would not remember, though. Time would not bring back the force of Shannon lowering the book and saying, with all the unused momentum of twenty years, I see them. Time would not recall her gently saying to me, Daniel, they're everywhere. Time refused that moment, her face, entirely.

The car righted itself—amazingly, unexpectedly—and we did not die. It was as if nothing had happened.

In some ways, that seemed right. There had been movement, but there were no real marks. Carolyn was crying, but that would pass. Only seconds were missing. Wouldn't driving to the shoulder, getting out of the car, stretching, take longer than the time it had taken to swerve, tremble briefly, and stop?

Still, in another way—in the only way, perhaps—it was wrong. Something *had* happened, if only the crafting of an absence. I knew when I met Shannon that she could walk the three flights to my apartment, that she could refuse drinks, hold books, ask questions, of course. But that she could say my name, Daniel, and have it different entirely. I didn't know that. I didn't know until my cousin began crying, until the car stopped, that I could never reach that moment again, that the sound was impossible.

Carolyn and I are lapsed Catholics. The same Carolyn who crossed herself—out of practice, going to the right before the left—after pulling the emergency brake. The same I who hoped to see Jesus—bearded, with soft eyes and a long robe—stepping out of the clouds when the car stopped. I never stopped looking up during my prayers, never ceded the idea that Heaven floats somewhere above us. As if God presides over a kingdom reachable by mountains or ladders. As if Heaven were a New World somehow missed by satellites and planes, and not a different universe entirely, one removed from the unwilling and inconsolable. What would it take, I sometimes wondered, to believe in God beyond fear or obligation? Why could I phrase the question only in terms of loss?

It wasn't God. It was Shannon's face. It was not dying. It was facing the wrong way on the highway, the cars coming closer, so that I could see *their* faces, some bothered, others aghast, one yelling through the window, saying something too far off to hear. The cars were coming closer, indifferent to time, or time indifferent to them, moving in normal time and slowing when they saw us in the middle of the highway, facing the wrong way. Something needed to happen.

Carolyn couldn't stop crying. It was strange how calm I was.

I didn't say anything to Carolyn. Instead I said to myself, Soon she will get it together. Soon we will drive to the side of the highway and get out of the car. Soon this will be over, I said, and this will become a day when something slightly out of the ordinary happened. That will happen soon.

But then I thought, Maybe that won't happen. Maybe instead, Shannon—unaware of the cars or indifferent to the lack of motion—will lower the book and say one more time, Daniel, I see them. Maybe her hand, shaking from a vision she never expected, will find my fingers and push them into the warm yellow wheat. Or maybe the crows, restless from a hundred years of false movement, will finally break into flight. Maybe the thin black birds— traveling swiftly, leaving empty spaces in the sky—will reach the low-hanging moon and settle there, wrap their wings around her hard white curves and talk about how the road below them, the one that is red and green, thrashes through the fields and doesn't end anywhere.

T-BONE CAPONE LOVES THE LADY ACE

In Islamorada the sky was blue and cloudless—perfect, except that neither of us could see the sun from the car, which Angela said was a bad sign. We had the windows down and the air conditioning on, a luxury we never allowed ourselves with my car. The rental was so clean it embarrassed me, as if my cluttered car were a testament to my reluctance to change or inability to recognize when I should. When I said this to Angela, she said my car needed a new muffler.

"Every time you go over thirty, it sounds like it's dying," she said.

"You're just saying that because this car is so quiet. This is the quietest car I've ever been in."

Angela turned off the radio and made a noise like she

was gargling without water, which sounded a lot like my car at forty-five miles per hour.

"That's good," I said.

"Where is the sun?" She undid her seat belt and turned around. "I haven't seen it since Miami."

We'd been driving for two hours, enough time for the spontaneity of the trip to approach frustration. We left after lunch, not sure how else to spend a long September Saturday. But when Angela ran to put on the one dress I'd ever bought her, and I scrambled to stuff clothes into a backpack, I was sure this was exactly what we needed: a long drive and a hotel stay far from the city. The rental car—a gift from the bus that ripped off my side mirror and cleanly scraped the car's door—seemed then a chariot sent to take us south. But the hotels looked dirty and expensive, and the sun was so far above us I felt directionless, and Angela sounded lonely.

"I didn't tell Stephanie we were going," Angela said.

"We didn't tell anyone. We filled the cat's bowl and we left."

"Why can't I get a signal?"

"There'll be reception at the hotel." I could fill the ice bucket and see when the pool closed.

"Let's stop at the next gas station. The car needs gas."

I always did what Angela wanted when it came to Stephanie because she was Angela's sister and she was dying. I read a poem once that pointed out how we're all dying, that every day we're dying, and it's only the speed at which we're dying that makes any difference. That poem stayed with me because I thought it was a remarkable

word to use: *speed*. What the poet knew, and Angela
came to understand when her sister got sick, you can only
understand when someone you love is dying. That was the
difference between Angela and me. She understood dying,
and I didn't. If I were a poet, I'd write a poem about that.
But I didn't know what to say to Angela, so I tried to give
her what she wanted and give her space, figuring someday
I would understand what she understood, and if I never
did, I would be more ignorant than most people and more
fortunate.

We stopped at the next gas station. On some keys
it seems there are more gas stations than houses, an
observation that's always amazed me. I stepped out of the
car to pump the gas, and when I turned around to talk to
Angela (no matter which one of us was filling the car, we
both got out, a tradition Angela started), I saw that she
was talking to a boy whose clothes were covered in oil
and waving her phone maniacally. I've never been good at
these things, but I'd say the boy was no older than twelve,
though he may have been as young as nine.

"Wheels and windows," the boy said. "One dollar."

"That won't be necessary," Angela said.

"One dollar," the boy repeated.

In my twenty-five years, I'd never heard anyone offer to
clean the wheels of a car. The idea agreed with me, maybe
because I'd always been too modest to ask for a shoe
shining, and this seemed as close as I would get. I reached
into my pocket.

"It's not even our car," Angela protested.

I handed the boy a dollar. It hadn't occurred to me that

the car wasn't ours and that, being a rental, the exterior was clean already.

"I'm getting a very faint signal." She shook her head, but I knew it relieved her to check on her sister. "Make sure he does the back windows."

"I do all the windows," the boy said.

He dropped to his knees and started scrubbing the hubcaps with a filthy rag.

"You're going to make them dirtier that way," I said.

"What do you know about it?" he asked without looking up.

It was true that I didn't know anything. I never even washed my own car. Two minutes later the tank was full and all four hubcaps were sparkling.

"What do you use on those wheels?" I asked.

The boy flashed me an impatient look and then bent over his bucket.

"It's not just water, is it?"

"I still have to do the windows," he said.

"Let me get out of your way."

On the phone, Angela was nodding with her lips pursed. She didn't do much of the talking when she called her sister.

"Tell you what," I said. "I'll give you another dollar if you tell me what you use on those wheels."

"No."

His refusal impressed me, so I offered him five.

The boy finished the windows before answering me, and when he stepped around the hood, it was clear just how dirty he was. His shirt and shorts were stained with grease, though bursts of faded bleach were visible around holes in the fabric. The thin hair on his arms and legs was speckled with dirt, and his knees were a uniform black. On his face were streaks of brown where he'd rubbed off sweat with his hand, and these patches were dry and flaking. He wore a teal Florida Marlins cap that was clearly new and important to him for the careful way he avoided sullying it.

"You can buy it in the station," the boy finally said. "It's nothing special."

I reached for a five-dollar bill and frowned to find nothing but two twenties.

"I'll make change," I said.

The boy waved me off. He picked up his bucket and rag, and as he walked to the next car, it grew obvious he would never accept money that wasn't commensurate to the work he put forth. It seemed a very dignified position for a boy to take, and I resented him for it. I considered offering him a full twenty, but that's the ridiculous person I can be.

Angela was impressed with the hubcaps when she came back.

"Everything he uses comes from the station," I said.

"That makes sense," she said.

"How's Stephanie?"

"It's a good day." On a good day, Stephanie didn't throw up and ate three meals. Those were the two requirements.

"It's early for dinner," I said.

"It's a good day so far."

True to form, Angela was in better spirits when we got back on the road.

"I know it doesn't make any sense," I said, "but earlier, when we couldn't find the sun, I felt like I didn't know where I was going."

"It's a two lane road." She pointed to Route 1. "But look! The sun is out now."

Was it a turn in the road, or just the time lapsed at the station, but *there* was the sun—a hazy yellow ball you couldn't look at for more than a second—hanging in the corner of the windshield.

"A good sign," Angela assured me. "Our fortune is improving."

"Maybe the boy put it there." At the time this struck me as clever, though it ended up doing more harm than good.

"They make me so sad."

"Not this boy. He's an entrepreneur and very dignified. I offered him five dollars, and he wouldn't take it."

"That was good of you."

"It was condescending, and he was too serious a worker to take it. He'll be a regular Rockefeller."

Angela considered the windshield. "Do you think he lives at the station?"

"I don't know where he lives. But he'll be all right. I could tell from five minutes that he was a serious worker." I hadn't realized until I began talking what an impression this boy had made on me.

"A boy that age shouldn't be cleaning windows all day."

I shifted in my seat and didn't say anything else because, of course, she was right on that point.

"Stephanie sounds terrible," Angela said. "Even when

she's happy, she sounds terrible."

"Was she happy on the phone?"

"Like I said, it's a good day."

According to the different things Angela read, Stephanie had anywhere from three months to two years left to live.

"But modern science." I had the great faith in modern science that people who used to be religious often have.

"Modern science is a wonderful thing." Somehow, the way she said this made my case seem even weaker.

I considered telling Angela about an article I'd read regarding a certain type of cancer, how things were different after this new and remarkable discovery, and how the whole medical community was surprised, but not really, because this was the forward direction medicine was moving in. I opened my mouth to tell her about it, but one look at her face convinced me to stay quiet and just reach for her hand, though she barely reached back, leaving her fingers limp in my palm. Her fingers, I remember, were damp like she'd been sweating.

"In any event, Stephanie told us to have a good time," Angela said.

"We will have a good time. We should stop soon. We should eat and get a little drunk." I turned to her. "You look beautiful in that dress. Did I tell you that already? You look great."

"There's something nice about a long drive in a beautiful dress. Not that I'm beautiful, but the dress is."

"It's—exotic."

"That's not right. I mean, I'm glad you're trying to put

yourself in my position, I do appreciate that, but it doesn't feel exotic. It's careless, in a way. In a good way."

"Careless as in no cares, no worries."

"Exactly." Angela tucked her bra strap back beneath her sleeve. "Not a thought in the world."

Angela *was* beautiful in that dress. She's a small woman, and her figure didn't always show in the things she wore, but this dress was a natural complement. Something about the cut, loose as it was, pointed to the curve in her calves and slenderness of her arms. The dress was a dark red, and this seemed to soften her skin everywhere, though nowhere more than her chest, which lightened in shades of brown down to the neckline. Even her fingers in this dress seemed exact, the only size they could be. When she first put on the dress, the precision of her hands—I should say the scale of her whole body, though it was her hands I noticed—shook me almost to tears. I thought then that her beauty exceeded my capacity to appreciate beauty, though I no longer believe this, not because she grew less beautiful, but because I know it was easier not to understand Angela than to try to understand her fully.

The hotel we settled on was a long two-story building with an expansive parking lot and tall sign with a pelican in a Hawaiian shirt. The pelican was holding a cocktail with an umbrella sticking out of it and smoking a half-finished cigarette. The hotel didn't appear to have a name, though the glowing green *vacancy* beneath the pelican left little doubt of the building's function. Neither Angela nor I consciously chose the hotel. I steered into the parking lot, as if magnetically drawn there, and when we stopped, Angela and I stepped out of the car in soundless agreement. We didn't have much to carry: There was the backpack with our clothes and my leather basketball, which I brought most places we went. I dribbled the ball on the way to the hotel lobby.

"You brought that thing?" Angela asked.

"I always bring it," I said.

"Leave it in the car."

"You think it will be safe?"

"We'll have bigger things to worry about if the car gets stolen."

I hadn't brought the basketball because I'm good at basketball or even because I like playing very much—I don't. I brought the basketball because I love shooting free throws. I seek out different hoops the way golfers search for far-flung courses. I've shot free throws on caged-in courts under subway tracks and in church parking lots, in air-conditioned gyms and on slanted driveways. The most consecutive free throws I ever made were twenty-seven on an outdoor court in Coral Springs, a number that strikes me as respectable. On three different occasions, I've gone as high as twenty-four. As a rule, I do not shoot for money, though I have been asked to enter bets on several occasions.

It didn't take long to check in. The woman behind the counter was cheery and accommodating, though she was old enough that I worried she might look sadly upon our lack of wedding bands. I paid with a credit card, and she handed us a key, which was attached to a seashell with the room number written in black magic marker.

"I'll pay you later," Angela said.

"Don't worry about it."

"You want to pay for the whole thing?" We didn't make a lot of money and split everything fifty-fifty.

"And dinner," I added hastily.

Angela stopped. She put her hands on her hips, but realizing the comic effect of this gesture, dropped them to her side. We were in the hallway in front of room number twelve. Our room was eighteen.

"I want to take you out. We're on vacation and we should get a decent dinner."

"You don't have to do that, Ray."

"I know, but it's important to me."

It was true that it was important to me, though it only became important when I offered. I was sure at that moment that if I could make Angela comfortable, I could make her happy. I decided to focus all my energy on making Angela happy, as if by narrowing my attention I could narrow hers, as well, and we could get back to the way things were before Stephanie got sick.

"All right, you can take me out." Angela leaned forward to kiss me, then plucked the key from my hand.

Room eighteen had two twin beds and a window overlooking the sand and grass lot behind the hotel. The walls were pink stucco, and the only decoration was an elaborately framed watercolor of two sailboats. Opposite the beds, an old television rested on a bureau. The wood of the bureau did not match the room.

"We can push the beds together," Angela said.

"I'd hoped for a little more luxury."

"But look at this bathroom." Angela opened the bathroom door and clicked on the light. "We have clean towels, soap in packages. We can keep this stuff, you know. They expect you to."

"I'm going to get some ice."

"We don't have anything to drink."

"I'll get a Coke. One Coke with ice, coming up."

I closed the door quietly on my way out. For a second, I considered leaving for good, not because I wanted to but because I enjoyed the momentary rush of freedom. I understood that this was a simple sensation, that if I left the freedom would quickly become a burden, and that I cared about Angela too much to abandon her. Still, it was an idea that came to me now and again and one I always welcomed with surprise, as you welcome an errant smile from a beautiful stranger whom you know you will never see again.

Of course, I didn't have any money for the vending machine. I considered getting change for my twenty, but the only option seemed the woman at the check-in desk, and her friendliness frightened me. I was scared she might want to talk and more scared I might not be able to stop. My emotions were fickle and volatile enough where I might even burst into tears in the right situation, and this was a humiliation I was unwilling to risk. So I paced up and down the hallway, trying to kill time, before knocking on our door with an expression that suggested an earnest effort had been carried out.

"No ice," Angela said.

"Or Coke."

"Let's get dinner."

I stepped into the room and glanced at the clothes scattered across the first twin bed.

"I call that bed," Angela said.

"Aren't you going to wear the dress you have on?"

"I thought you might want to change your shirt."

I put on the shirt, though I didn't remember packing it.

"Did you call Stephanie?" I asked.

"She's probably sleeping, or maybe she took a walk up the hallway like you did."

Stephanie's walks were desperate affairs that ended quickly, often with Stephanie breathing hard in her apartment foyer. I felt a sudden shame for my own vitality.

"I'm ready when you're ready," I said.

"Ready, ready, ready," Angela said, swooping her purse off the bed.

It had started to rain, one of those impossible to anticipate Florida sprinklings where the sun never leaves and clouds never appear. The rain was light and sticky and in the evening glare almost invisible, so that stepping into it was like stepping into a spider web. The entire walk to the car Angela floated her hands above her head, as if to warn her hair against frizzing. I followed a step or two behind, watching the rain slide down Angela's arms and wondering where we might eat.

"This ball." Angela pointed to my basketball through the passenger side window. "You bring it more places than you bring me."

I fumbled through my pocket.

"What if I got rid of it?" Angela asked. "What if threw

it in the trash?"

"Don't talk crazy talk." I unlocked the doors.

"What if I destroyed this basketball? What would you do?"

"I suppose I would have to leave you. It would represent a profound lack of respect."

"It really would." Angela seemed pleased. "You love this basketball."

"I do."

"But not more than you love me."

"No, not more than that."

"If your love for me is a ten, what is your love for this basketball?"

"My love for you is an eleven." I started the car.

Like so many things, my love is rooted almost entirely in context. There's nothing exceptional about the actual ball, save its durability, even if it exists now devoid of grip and with a slow, consistent leak. When I first received the ball, I would shoot free throws for hours, creating scenarios in which each shot determined a specific conclusion: If I make this shot, the Heat win the championship; if I make this shot, with my eyes closed, Erika goes to Homecoming with me; if I make this shot, hitting no part of the rim, the University of Florida accepts me. From an early age we want justice but, not yet being adults, have almost no control over its implementation. What is fair punishment for a broken window? In free throws, I had instant justice and absolute accountability, provided I committed myself to the system, which I did. Little matter if results followed; it was the system I was faithful to and the system I remembered.

"Where to?" Angela asked.

"I was thinking south," I said, choosing that direction because it was an easier turn out of the parking lot.

"That boy at the gas station mentioned somewhere."

I was struck with unexpected jealousy. "Does he work there, too?"

"All he said was that if I was sticking around, I should try the Happy Boar."

"Is that a pun?"

The Happy Boar wasn't hard to find. A few miles down the road stood a large sign directing cars to the restaurant. The coral road was narrow and overgrown in places, so that palm fronds slapped loudly against the car. At one point it got so bad we had to roll up the windows, and when I opened my mouth to complain about scratches, Angela placed a finger in front of my lips and whispered, "It's all right, it's all right."

The road ended in a parking lot, which was full of cars. From the outside, the Happy Boar was an unremarkable building: short and red and absent windows. The door was red, as well, and would be easy to miss were it not for the yellow boar painted at eye level. Unlike the pelican from the hotel, this was realism at its finest. Nothing about the boar appeared particularly happy, and I wondered if the restaurant's name was an irony I wasn't privy to, an inside joke among the locals. I considered knocking before entering—as if the building were some Prohibition relic, and I needed a password—but Angela pushed forward with confidence.

The inside was glorious! Thick tables circled around

an open floor, where drunken patrons vied for the crowd's
attention in a sort of karaoke/street performer hybrid.
A man in a wool suit stumbled through Bob Marley
songs while another man juggled packs of cigarettes. The
bar filled with colored drinks, which people seemed to
grab at random, littering the bar with money that sank
into the puddles the drinks left behind. At the back of
the restaurant, doors opened onto a wooden deck that
stretched across the surprising ocean and under a sun just
beginning its languid descent. A waitress with waist-length
hair shuffled between the inside and outside, emptying
ashtrays and taking orders.

"Table for two," Angela said when the waitress passed
us.

"Wherever you want, babe."

Angela chose a table along one of the walls because she
was scared the rain might pick up outside. The menu was
short—dominated by appetizers and mixed drinks—and
reasonably priced. I wanted a hamburger.

"What should I get?" Angela asked.

"You like chicken sandwiches."

"I mean to drink. I'm ready for a drink."

I'd never seen Angela have more than two drinks. She
enjoyed a drink now and again, sometimes even sought
one out, but she always lost interest after an hour or so.
There had been a handful of times after a long night
with friends, or at the end of a party, where I turned
glazed and spinning to find Angela sitting absolutely still
with her hands folded in her lap, her eyes fixed on some
insignificant object, a glass or chair. In those moments

she never said anything until I did, and there was always something embarrassing about my voice: the tilt to it, or the urgency that seemed so inappropriate beside her calm. There was a seriousness to Angela then, but a sort of self-contained sadness, as well, an unhappiness that seemed to spring entirely from within her, so that when she finally responded it was regretfully, as if she had seen something she wished she hadn't—something she felt bad for even acknowledging. It happened before Stephanie got sick but more frequently afterward. Anytime it happened we would leave, and in the morning she was always fine.

"I'm getting a beer," I said. "Something local."

"I'm getting—" Angela dragged her finger down the laminated menu. "A Green Hemingway. No, a Coral Sunrise."

"What's that?"

"It's everything. Very strong."

"I'll get a big beer."

The waitress came by and took our order. She was a plain looking woman, though her hair really was something. You couldn't help but admire it.

"I bet it takes her an hour to dry it," Angela said.

"I bet it takes two hours."

"It was a good idea to come here."

"I know." I tapped our menus against the table and stacked them behind the napkin dispenser. "I realize how—"

"It's all right."

I dragged the salt and pepper shakers into the center of the table and pushed them apart ominously, as if they were enemies.

"Jesus." Angela pushed her chair back. "It's that boy again."

I turned around but didn't see anything. I stood to get a better angle but still couldn't find him.

"On the dance floor," Angela said. "In the hat, look!"

The boy was barely recognizable. His oil-soaked clothes had been replaced by a sharp blue suit, and he'd exchanged his Marlins cap for a menacing blue fedora with a long purple feather (what bird this could have come from, I can't imagine). Beneath his suit he wore a clean white shirt and a yellow tie that stretched well past his waist. He wasn't singing yet but marching up and down the floor, staring at his microphone and waiting for the music to start. His face was clean now, though brown crescents were still visible beneath his fingernails, a detail I could only notice when we left our seats to join the crowd forming around the clearing. Small as she is, Angela had to stand on her toes to get a good look, and she waved her hand back and forth, trying to catch the boy's attention to let him know we'd come to the Happy Boar, after all.

The boy raised his right hand, and the crowd quieted amidst muffled laughter. He announced a song, and I cheered along with the crowd, though I'd never heard of the song before.

"He looks so different here." Angela kept looking over her shoulder to see if our drinks had come.

"The crowd seems to like him."

"They love him. He's a star." Angela spotted the waitress with a drink tray and took a step toward her. "Let me just see if these are ours."

"She'll leave them on the table."

"I know. I'll be right back."

Without Angela, I pushed a little closer to the clearing. The first bright notes of the song were streaming through the speakers, and the boy continued to stare at his microphone, tapping his foot to the simple, electronic drumbeat. The song crescendoed slightly, and the boy dropped to one knee and stared at the ceiling, holding the microphone just beneath his chin to the endless delight of two middle-aged women beside me. I've tried to describe his voice with difficulty before and I can say only that it surprised me, that it surprised many people and didn't surprise others. I wouldn't call it a good voice, though it wasn't unpleasant to listen to, a necessary complement to his dancing, where he won the crowd. But even that's not right because it wasn't dancing. It was *strategic moving*, a way of maximizing the attention given to his arm gestures, pacing, even jumping. He knew the words by heart and understood the exact moment to enter and leave a song. Still, there was something mechanical—even static—about the performance, and it occurred to me that he was a student of karaoke in the same way that he was a student of hubcaps. With both, he had taken a thoughtless art and brought not passion but discipline. I had the sudden urge to shoot free throws with him, to find a hoop and work on his form for hours.

At the end of the song, the boy made a sweeping bow toward his Marlins cap, which was turned upside down on the floor before him. Of course, it was unusual to solicit money after a karaoke performance, but people had loose bills and they wasted little time stuffing his cap. I turned around to gauge Angela's reaction, but there were only the two drinks at the table. She wasn't by the restrooms, nor was she at the bar, where one of the bartenders looked over the crowd with so much pride and satisfaction I wondered if he might be the boy's father. Unless the boy really did live at the gas station. But then where did he keep the blue suit, how did he iron his shirt? And what if he didn't have parents at all, if he cleaned hubcaps by day and sang karaoke at night, hoarding his money and sleeping where he could? The question didn't fill me with sadness so much as confusion. That Stephanie could get sick and die made sense; I could see that, even if I couldn't feel it. But that this boy could live—somehow, my mind couldn't grasp it.

The boy wanted to do a second song, and nobody minded. I stared at him as he prepared, searching for some suggestion of sadness, even boredom, but he was all business. I suppose it was part of the act, that whether he realized it or not—and, probably, he did—his seriousness only made him stranger and more interesting. Perhaps he understood that the sobriety that made him an efficient cleaner benefited him in karaoke as well, though for different reasons. But what a combination! Surely it was the result of a father or uncle—I was certain it was a man—who saw past his own laziness to the profitability of an unusually diligent child in an unusual place. How badly I wanted to rescue this boy and how doomed it made me feel. Would you believe me if I told you I felt closer to that father or uncle than I did the boy?

The boy finished the second song, then a third, and all

the while I stood among the gathering, not because I didn't know where Angela was but because I didn't know what to say. I knew that Stephanie was nearing the end of a litany of complaints. I knew that throughout the conversation Stephanie was gently punishing Angela, reminding her of how irresponsible it had been to leave. Stephanie would never say it—she didn't have to—but what if something happened, if she became so suddenly ill she couldn't take care of herself? Such things, of course, were not impossible. Not even unlikely. For her part, Angela was apologetic without apologizing—everything she said a slight concession. There's nothing to be sorry about, she would say to me later that night, gradually constructing the argument she couldn't bring herself to deliver to her sister. I listened respectfully. I didn't disagree. Would I have helped her more had I challenged a thing she said?

After the third song, the boy picked up his hat and walked to the bar for a Coke. The next time I looked at the bar he wasn't there. I never saw him again.

Angela was sitting at our table when I got back.

"Have you been waiting long?" I asked, though I knew she couldn't have been there more than a minute.

"Try this." She lifted her drink toward my face.

"I'm good."

"Well, this is good." She took a long sip, then quietly set down her drink. "That boy was something, wasn't he?"

"I can't understand him."

"What's there to understand?"

I sat and drank my beer.

"We should order," Angela said. "Maybe I will get a

chicken sandwich."

Angela ordered for us when the waitress came by again.

We didn't talk much for the rest of dinner. I didn't want to ask Angela about Stephanie, and Angela didn't want to tell me about her. I got another beer, and Angela studied the drink menu carefully, though she asked for water. The later we stayed, the busier the Happy Boar became, and by the time we left, a live band had started on the deck. As we made our way out, a swarm of teenagers rushed inside with loud plans to get the band to play the theme song from *Shaft*.

"It's not even late," Angela said. "Do you want another round?"

"We don't have to do that."

"We can't be far from a bar. These places are lined with them."

"I'm ready to head back. All the driving, you know."

Angela ran ahead of me and turned around in the middle of the parking lot. She danced a little, trying to get me to smile, and I pushed out a few clumsy moves, which only made her work harder. It often went this way: one of us lapsing suddenly into dejection and the other trying desperately to cheer up the first person, regardless of how frustrated we both might be.

"I can't dance," I said.

"No rhythm," Angela agreed sadly.

"I tried. A little, anyhow."

"Not really." Angela smiled at a young couple walking to the restaurant.

"I'll get another drink."

"Ray, check this out."

I walked past the couple to Angela. As far as I could tell, she was staring at a pair of dumpsters.

"Isn't it terrific?" she said.

I peered in closer and saw that the name *T-Bone Capone* had been spray-painted across two dumpsters. In general, the artistry of graffiti doesn't impress me, and this job was no different.

"It's a good name," I said. "I mean, it's original."

"No, *look*." Angela grabbed my wrist and walked to the dumpsters. She pointed to the wall behind them then looked at me expectantly.

"*T-Bone Capone Loves the Lady Ace*," I read.

"I love that. That could be me: the Lady Ace."

"Wouldn't you be the Lady Angel? Or just Angel—isn't Lady Angel sexist?"

"You don't get it at all."

"I went to school with a guy named Travis who we called T-Wheels."

"I know you think it's stupid, and normally I would too, but tonight I like it." Angela scanned the rest of the wall and paused when she saw a basketball hoop drilled into the far end of the wall.

"It's about the right height," I said. "The rim's a little bent."

"You should get your ball."

"Now?"

"Isn't that why you drag it everywhere?"

I didn't think about it—I just walked to the car. It wasn't until I was on my way back, walking past people stumbling to their cars, that I considered what I was doing. The risks, as I saw them, were minimal: Angela might get bored, or, hampered by the two drinks and angle of the rim, I might miss more than I made. Then I thought of how I'd wanted to make Angela happy, and it seemed that this was in the right vein, that if she wanted me to shoot free throws, I could shoot them. If she wanted to be the Lady Ace, I could be T-Bone Capone.

The ball bounced poorly on the coral, so I only dribbled it a few times before taking it under my arm and walking beneath the hoop. I jumped and gave the rim a slight tug. It was bent forward, to be sure, but nothing I couldn't adjust to. There was no netting, and while that throws some people off, it doesn't bother me. I took exactly seventeen-and-a-half steps from the wall and dug a faint line across the coral with my heel. For show, I licked my forefinger and thrust it into the air. My hands were sticky from the beer glasses, and mosquitoes circled around my wrist. I took the ball into my hands and rubbed them dry. Never one for elaborate rituals, I bent my knees and made the first shot easily.

"Bravo." Angela clapped. She seemed vaguely surprised any of this was happening. She retrieved the ball off one bounce and politely walked it to me.

"It's not a bad hoop," I said. "I've seen worse in gyms."

I made the second shot. A fortuitous bounce sent the ball back to me, so I lined up and hit the third shot, as well.

"You can't miss," Angela said.

"Three shots isn't anything."

"You should do that thing."

I gathered the ball and turned it in my hands. I bounced it once and then made a fourth free throw, the purest shot to that point.

"You know what I mean," she said. "Where you pick what you're shooting for."

"I don't do that anymore."

"Make the next shot and I'll give you a kiss."

"Low stakes."

Angela gasped in delight. She studied the ball as it tripped over the coral then turned her eyes to my face, which I imagine revealed some variation of confidence and amusement—not smugness so much as contentment. I was feeling good, the best I'd felt all day, and the spontaneity of *this* is what I'd been looking for since Miami. The air was heavy with that raw, almost lustful smell seafood and liquor can create, and I remember looking at Angela with embarrassment. When I bent to pick up the ball, I stared at my own sandaled feet and the crushed beer cans scattered across the lot like weeds. I saw how the powdered chalk of the coral had crept up Angela's calves. The sun had set, and the few lights in the parking lot were just beginning to sputter on, but the fifth shot wasn't difficult to make.

"Double or nothing?" Angela asked, handing me the ball.

I nearly missed the sixth shot—the ball bounced twice off the rim—and Angela shouted before placing a prudish kiss on each of my cheeks.

"Shoot for Stephanie now."

"She's not here," I said, disappointed at this turn.

"No, shoot *for* her. A month per shot." Angela kicked

the ball to me. "Make two shots, she lives two months. That sort of thing."

"I can't do that, Angela."

"Sure you can. Look." She pointed to the hoop, and her voice rose slightly. "You haven't missed all night."

I shifted the ball under my arm and looked at Angela, waiting for her to take it back or laugh—anything, really, to change what she'd asked for. She didn't say a word, though. She scratched her forearm and looked at the hoop.

"It's okay if you miss," Angela said. "It's just a game."

"I realize that."

"So, go ahead."

"I'm not shooting. Not for that."

Angela didn't move.

"What if we make it years instead of months?" I asked.

"It has to be realistic."

I took the ball into my hands. I understood the rim now, and my muscles felt warm and relaxed. There was a chance I could make another fifteen or twenty before missing.

"Here's the thing," I said. "I'm going to miss. Probably not this shot, but soon."

"That is the thing."

"So I'm only going to shoot because it's a game, which I haven't played in years. When I miss, which I will, it won't matter."

"We agree that it's just a game," Angela said.

I took the first shot quickly, before I could worry over it too much. The ball slammed into the backboard then fell into the hoop as a sort of afterthought.

"October," Angela said.

The next two shots went in, and Angela followed them glibly, almost disinterestedly, with November and December. When I made the fourth shot, Angela shouted, "Happy New Year!"

"I can't do this anymore."

"You have to. It's important."

I look at this moment now as one of my weakest, for there are times when I feel bad about a shot, when I'm nearly certain that I'll miss, and this was one of them. I looked at the hoop knowing I would miss and I shot anyway because I didn't know what else to do. I held the ball longer than usual, and as soon as it left my fingers, I could see that it was high and off-center. Angela, who had little interest in basketball and had never once seen me shoot, knew I'd missed, as well. I say this not because she told me later or because I had a supernatural sense for the moment, but because as soon as I released the ball I turned to Angela, and her expression told me everything. I never saw the ball clank off the rim, I only heard it—a flat, easily identifiable sound.

"There you have it," she said.

"I'm sorry, Angela."

"It's not your fault, so don't feel bad."

"It's not your fault, either."

"Of course not." Angela bent to pick up the ball.

"Drinks on me."

"I'm tired, Ray." She looked up and reached for my arm. "Let's head back."

Stephanie lived another two years. The end of the

trip marked the beginning of a long upswing for her, a time where, briefly, it seemed she might come out of it completely. The optimism was terrifying because it was also impossible. Still, when I read her obituary, the death seemed both anticlimactic and unfathomable, something I'd always known and the last thing I would have expected. Without thinking, I called the only number I've ever had from Angela, but nobody picked up, and the voicemail was wrong.

We stayed together four more months after the trip. I didn't realize until Angela left, until I'd exhausted my pleas for her to stay with surprising swiftness, that the system I'd formed at twelve was sound, only I had it backward. With practice, I could control my shot. What I was shooting for—the circumstances I created with agonizing precision—I could never predict.

OPEN HOUSE

Josie loved the kitchen. She loved the enormous windows and the marble counters and especially the cabinets, which were the only color they could possibly be. The appliances were silver. They looked like beautiful new weapons. Josie loved the tile so much she felt bad wearing her shoes. She almost took them off, but the realtor assured her this wasn't necessary. Tim shot her a vicious look. The look announced he could do without the theatrics, but Josie couldn't help herself.

She said, "This tile can't possibly be original." She was eager for the realtor to assure her it was.

Tim wandered out of the kitchen and into the backyard. He lit a cigarette philosophically. Josie watched from the enormous window.

"That means he's thinking," Josie assured a woman she'd never met. "That means he loves it, in his way."

"What's not to love?" the woman wanted to know.

Josie opened a cabinet and gazed into its emptiness.

"The tile is from the twenties," the realtor said.

Josie joined Tim in the backyard. It was more space than they needed. She tried to communicate this with a modest shrug, but he wasn't looking at her so much as the gigantic palm that stood on the edge of the lawn like a watchtower. It was twice the height of the house, probably. The other palms shirked away in embarrassment. She was embarrassed for them.

"I'm not enjoying this," he said quietly.

"Try to see things the Agency's way."

"That's the way I've been trying to see them."

She looked at the window. The sun prevented her from seeing who was watching. She waved, anyhow. When she turned around, Tim was by the palm, running a hand up and down the trunk. She stepped over a sprinkler head. She put a hand on his back. His shoulders twitched, and he moved his neck, but he didn't turn around.

"They're watching," she said.

The kitchen was empty now. She moved to the living room, where the curtains were open. Where sun luxuriated in the chairs and stretched across the single elegant rug. She swept a finger over the rug and didn't find a single hair. Josie put her arm around the sun and leaned into the couch. There was no television. She stared up the stairs. She didn't see anything and didn't hear anything. When the door opened, she sprung off the couch. She

straightened her hair, though it was straight. Her blouse
was finer than any other blouse she owned. Same with her
skirt. Same with her shoes.

Tim had combed his hair. He'd shaven attentively;
there was no question about what was his beard and what
wasn't. His shirt was tucked into his pants. She wasn't sure
if she liked the two buttons undone below his neck.

He said, "Let's see upstairs."

Not *go*, see. It was a nice touch. She followed him. The
couple upstairs couldn't agree on the bedroom windows.
The woman thought they were too large, while the man
thought that was the best thing about them. Josie couldn't
bear to listen to either opinion. She tried to open the
largest window, but it wouldn't open. The woman nodded
knowingly. Tim stared into the backyard. Somehow, the
palm looked even taller up here. Closer too. She could
touch it, if the window opened. The couple left the
bedroom, but Josie and Tim stayed.

The realtor found them sitting on the bed. There was
no box spring, just a mattress. Josie felt like she was in
college, though she had a perfectly serviceable bed in
college, though she went to a commuter school and came
home every weekend to see her mother, who was dying or
at least pretending to die. At home, Josie's bed couldn't be
softer. Tim didn't finish college. It was a subject.

The realtor said, "Do you have any questions?"

Tim said, "All I have is questions."

Too quickly, the realtor smiled. He led them into
the bathroom. Josie ran the faucet until the water turned
warm. She couldn't think of what else to do.

"Can I ask you about the tree?" Tim asked.

"The tree?"

"Does it come with the house?"

The realtor looked to Josie.

"Or does it belong to the house behind?" Tim asked.

"It's right on the edge, but it *leans* into this property."

The tree was hard to ignore. Every window in the house framed the tree, and it looked the same from every angle. It looked tall. It looked dangerous. Josie couldn't help but imagine the tree crashing into the roof. She braced herself. She almost held her head. It hurt in advance.

"When was the roof redone?" she asked.

"Everything is original," the realtor said. "Well, not the tub. Not the wiring. But structurally."

"It's a lovely house."

There was nothing else to say in the bathroom. They walked around the perimeter of the second bedroom. They appreciated the natural light. They didn't even consider turning on a light, though the switches looked very modern, though the light bulbs were environmentally sensitive. The realtor spoke in a voice that wasn't so intimate the other couple couldn't hear. They huddled in the center of the room, pretending to be oblivious. The man put his hand on the woman's arm, and the woman put her hand over his hand, but these gestures didn't add up to what they were supposed to.

Josie stretched her arms, as if to say, The couch will go here. She stretched her legs on the couch. She left on her shoes. She looked for the sun, but it hadn't made its way up the stairs. That made sense. She was tired too. Without her having to say anything, Tim nodded, and her heart jumped. She made room for him on the couch. Why should it bother her that everyone was watching?

The realtor looked like he was thinking of joining her on the couch, but there was no room for him. She had to be careful. She was thinking like Tim, and this kind of thinking had put them in trouble. She got off the couch. When the realtor asked if it was time to draw up a contract, Josie agreed it was that time. Tim was silent. He gave the realtor a look that suggested he'd been won over. That, really, he would be a fool to argue after what they'd seen. It took tremendous restraint for Josie not to check the couple's reaction, but she didn't, and they were gone. The realtor put his hands in his pockets. Tim opened his mouth, and the realtor dug his hands deeper. There was no bottom to the realtor's pockets.

Josie looked down the stairs as if courageously awaiting her sentencing. She sensed Tim watching from the railing. She sensed the realtor watching Tim. She had another ten minutes. Without looking at her watch, she knew that. She wasn't sure what Tim remembered. It wasn't like she could ask with everyone watching. She glided down the stairs to the table. It was the only piece of furniture besides the couch. She wondered if this was the best way to sell a house, but what did she know about selling houses? She'd brought her own pen. She'd brought her own calculator. She laid them on the table.

Tim joined her. He put a hand over the calculator, but it might have been her hand. They might have been sitting

down for dinner. They might have been sitting down to
have a serious conversation about one of their children
or the gutters or a new position in Tampa-St. Pete. They
would have two children who would be above average at
something artistic or a minor sport.

The realtor put his hand on the edge of the table.
"Maybe not this time," he said.

Josie looked up.

"Maybe we need some time—I don't know—to
regroup."

"Right," Josie said.

The realtor moved to the front door. He held it open.
Josie waited for another couple to arrive, but nobody was
arriving. She stuffed her pen and calculator into her purse.
She checked her hair in the window but couldn't see
anything.

"If not regroup then something," the realtor said.

"Of course," Tim said.

"You understand."

Josie forgot how nice the front steps looked. So easy to
take steps for granted. She relished each of them. She used
the handrail not out of necessity but for pleasure. It was
cold, even though it was ninety-five degrees outside. Why
was the grass so green? It didn't look like grass so much
as bad carpeting. The little black sprinkler heads looked
like landmines. She braced for an explosion. Tim walked
down the driveway like they were about to speed off in
a powerful car. Like this house wasn't half as good as the
next one they were seeing and nobody was even watching.

There were two cars in the driveway. She was glad

they weren't hers, though Tim's car was too small. You couldn't fit anything. Her legs hurt just thinking of folding into Tim's miniature car. He hustled down the driveway without looking to see where she was, and she wondered what the realtor was thinking. Was he disappointed? Did he expect that on some level? She didn't know what to expect. She thought she needed to think.

Tim was halfway down the street. She caught up to him but didn't touch him. She didn't have to. He quickened his pace. He said there wasn't a lot of time, and there wasn't. Nobody had to tell Josie that. She quickened her pace until she passed him. She spun around, sort of jogging backward, but he didn't smile. He said it would be you know what if they didn't get to the next house in the next five minutes, and it really would be. So she moved. The next house looked like the last house. It looked like all the houses.

The realtor looked like all the realtors. She welcomed them into the living room, where two couples uncomfortably shared a couch. One couple was much taller than the other. The tall couple looked past the small couple, as if they felt bad for being so tall. The small couple wasn't even that small. The realtor couldn't stop moving. Josie wanted to tell her to just *breathe* but of course Josie could never do a thing like that. She sat in the empty chair, and Tim stood behind her, listening. He listened to how new the bathroom was and how old the tiles were and how much space there was in the backyard, or so Josie assumed. She couldn't listen to anything.

Why should there be anything unusual about her?

There were a million Josies. She wasn't better than the worst of them. There were a million Tims. She looked at Tim as if looking at another version—an inferior copy—and she didn't like what she saw. But this version was focused. You had to give this version that. He leaned forward at the right times. The other couples noticed he was a serious buyer. He had twenty percent to put down. When the realtor stopped talking, he would ask the right questions and open his mouth at the wrong answers.

But was she the dutiful wife? She felt less than that. Mostly, she felt hungry. Could the others see her appetite? They were masterful in their disguises. The men were even more elusive than the women. The men looked like they all had more important appointments coming. They all had twenty percent to put down and they had the right questions. They didn't notice Tim because he was remarkable; they simply noticed he was one of them. Tim crossed his arms with casual disinterest.

The realtor led everyone into the kitchen. She leaned against the wall like a tour guide waiting for her group to make its way through the exhibit. She opened various drawers not to find anything but to keep her hands moving. Her hands found a bottle opener. Her hands found a spoon. She waved it like a wand over the marble counters, but there was no magic in this wand. The sun laid the room bare.

"Well, we should get started," the realtor said.

"I understand the tiles predate the Great Depression," one of the men said.

"They were flown in from Mauritius," the other man said.

"You mean Morocco," one of the women said.

"That makes more sense," the other woman said.

"The faucet is brand new," Tim said. "No, the faucet—"

"The faucet is beautiful," Josie said.

Only it wasn't beautiful. It wasn't anything. It was a faucet. Anyone could see that. Josie couldn't help but nudge it with her elbow. She couldn't help but smack it and take a step back before looking around wildly to see who noticed. Everyone was politely unaware. The realtor opened a cabinet to reveal a television. There wasn't supposed to be a television. This wasn't going according to plan. She looked to Tim, who looked past her completely, who followed the television like it was the most important thing in the world, which at that moment it was.

At the start of the last century, a courageous developer saw promise where everyone else saw swamp. Where everyone saw mosquitoes and fever and maybe even Indians, this developer saw a place where opportunistic Americans could plant roots for a reasonable price. It went without saying that the developer was bringing a kind of dream to a people unjustly denied the future they deserved. An unruly tangle of green gave way to a clean lawn with synchronized sprinklers, and a man in a khaki suit walked barefoot toward the camera. He was the developer's descendant in spirit. He wouldn't have looked uncomfortable in a Panama hat, though the director had declared this a step too far. The director had made a series of shrewd decisions, such as not showing any houses. The director was creating an aura. It had more to do with the house you wanted. Josie looked around the house she was

standing in. She looked at Tim to see if he remembered
what happened next, but he'd never forgotten, and she
shouldn't have either.

The man without the Panama hat was smiling. He
looked so happy. Tim wasn't quite so convincing, but he
was good. Josie didn't have a sense of how good or bad she
was. She thought, probably, that the other couples were
better. The realtor was superior. She watched the video like
it was a piece of art, like the man without the Panama hat
was among the singular influences of his era. The realtor
watched the video and the couples simultaneously. Here
was a woman who knew what she wanted and what she
was supposed to want. Josie couldn't help but admire her.

They were in the backyard. They were at the top of
the stairs. They were congratulating the short couple on
the sale, a little crestfallen but also genuinely happy to see
someone else, in the same position, happy. She tried to
gauge how happy the short couple was. She couldn't go on
looks. The situation demanded a more delicate approach.
She took a step closer. Nobody else was so bold! She had
to give herself credit for that. She might not be as skilled
or even beautiful as the other women but she also wasn't
as bashful. Unless she was making a terrible mistake.
She almost took a step back but she didn't want to look
weak. She turned to Tim, who was standing precisely
where he was supposed to stand. When had he become so
competent? It hardly seemed fair.

The room was empty. Even Tim was gone. Josie went
from room to room looking for him, but nobody was there.
A calm passed through her. Finally, she had time to think.

She sat on the floor. There was no furniture, not even a couch, not even a bed! Surely, this was no way to sell a house. The window before her opened to a large backyard. It was so empty. Josie stood. She walked through the front door. She walked to where the cars had been, then started walking home. It was hot. It was always hot. She reviewed her performance. Had it been credible? She thought it had. But had it been persuasive? That was a tougher question. If she was being honest, she would have to admit it hadn't been terribly persuasive. She would have to concede that, on a fundamental level, she'd failed. Of course, only so much was in her control. There was everyone else. Still, the sun felt more piercing, and the walk felt longer.

Her apartment was at the top of a long flight of stairs. She barely made her way up before collapsing onto the couch. Her roommate Liz—one of the world's truly annoying people—had left various boxes open on the table. Josie lit a cigarette, though she'd agreed not to do this. She looked through the boxes but didn't find anything interesting. She found the earrings Liz claimed not to have stolen. Josie resented what a bad liar Liz was and considered ways to get back at her. Spitefully, Josie put on the earrings, which she didn't even like anymore.

She put out her cigarette in an empty Diet Coke can. She stared at the blinds. They were always closed. She lit another cigarette. Liz wouldn't be home for a long time. Josie could use the spray. She looked for the spray, but this simple task exhausted her, and she sprawled across the living room floor. Her legs were still burning from sprinting up the stairs. She had an idea. It didn't have to be a good idea. She recognized that now.

Any minute she would put her idea into motion, but for now she could lie on the carpet. She hated the carpet except when she was lying on it. Then it was perfect. Then she could stay there all afternoon. She'd never noticed how brown the ceiling was. Maybe the brown spots were leaks. Maybe the people above her were lying in overflowing tubs. She couldn't remember the last time she'd taken a bath. But she didn't have a tub and she didn't have time for baths, not when there was this idea to put into motion. She leaned forward. She didn't sit all the way up, not yet.

Josie reached for the phone. She tried to remember the number, but it escaped her completely. She lit another cigarette and repeated three times that nothing was out of control until she let it be out of control. She sat all the way up and changed her clothes to something more comfortable. Something more her. It was easy to confuse who she was for what she did, but isn't that true of everyone? It's true of a lot of people. True for Liz. True for Tim. She stared at the phone. She remembered the number and already she was trying to forget it. This was why Liz said nobody trusted her. Liz didn't say nobody trusted her but she implied it. Well, Liz didn't say a lot of things.

Now Josie was on her feet. She was making something to eat. She never ate. Step One: Josie would take better care of herself. Step Two: Josie would stop letting other people bully her. Step Three: Josie wasn't sure. She had to think. She called Tim. He didn't pick up but he was home. She imagined him picking up his phone and seeing the number and lowering the phone slowly. She wasn't finished with Step Two, not until she spoke to Tim about what had happened. Not until she let Liz know where she was coming from, just how unacceptable things had become. She could be persuasive. It was her job to be. She was on the phone again. She was leaving the kind of message a person couldn't easily ignore. She was putting down the phone and waiting for his apology. After this, it would have to be a good one. Better than he was capable of, maybe. Josie was standing alone in her living room. She was getting used to it.

So she wasn't cut out for this work. She would sit at the kitchen table and draft her resignation letter to the Agency. She wouldn't show up to the next house. The kitchen table wasn't even in the kitchen. It was in the living room. There wasn't even a real kitchen. The little electric stove hadn't worked in weeks. She blamed her weight loss on its collapse. Plus, the stress from Tim. She might as well move on without him. Why wander through empty houses when she could sell makeup or wait tables or answer phone calls or make phone calls?

Can I interest you in a limited time offer? For this short time only, we have the most beautiful pans. We have the most beautiful tulips. We have the very best prosthetic limbs. You have been selected to receive the first thirty days free. If you choose at any point to cancel—listen, you would be crazy to cancel. This really is a limited offer. You really have been selected. I wouldn't just call anyone.

CHARLESTON FOR BREAKFAST

I was halfway into town when I decided what a bad idea it had been to leave my shift at the factory early. At the time, I was a security guard. I was twenty-two years old. Between midnight and seven my obligations were straightforward: Stay awake and don't go anywhere. What I did was sit in a chair, drink coffee, occasionally stroll the parking lot, and smoke cigarettes. Plus, this was a good paying job. So when I found myself in my car at five o'clock in the morning because I'd run out of cigarettes and was dying for a donut, I figured it was over, that I'd blown it again.

I forgot about all of this as I was sitting in Staunton Donut, putting the finishing touches on my second honey-glazed. Staunton Donut was great because it was right next door to the only twenty-four-hour gas station in town, and that's where I bought my cigarettes. By five-thirty everything seemed perfect, and I suppose that's why I decided to wake up my girlfriend, though it wasn't long before I remembered what I'd done and realized she wasn't going to be hot on me losing my job for a nicotine and sugar fix.

In my head I tried to justify why I'd left work, tried to come up with a good reason to give Emma, but I didn't have one. I'd had the job for seven weeks and I couldn't take another hour of it. During a few of my shifts I'd seen some deer, yellow-eyed and quiet, tiptoe into the lot like they knew they were doing something wrong, and I thought, Who are you to go wherever you want? I'm the security guard. That's trespassing. One time I threw a rock at one and missed its hind legs by a few feet. It was a rotten thing to do, I know, but it killed me thinking those deer could prance all over town, that they could get up and go anywhere, while I was stuck in a plastic chair, clicking an orange flashlight.

So I drove to Emma's house, smoking with the window cracked, watching the bashful way shadows sit in the darkness. I don't mind saying I was in a good mood. I've never been one to let losing a job ruin a good cigarette, or a date with Emma. Unfortunately, Emma didn't know we had a date, and when I delivered three hard knocks to her bedroom window, her first thoughts couldn't have been good. She pulled up the blinds and opened the window and when she saw it was me, she said, "You almost gave me a heart attack. What are you doing here?"

"I got off early."

"Oh, Mark."

Emma's a smart woman and even half asleep she knew damn well that nobody gets off the graveyard shift early and that I was out of work again.

"I'm sorry."

"Give me a second," she said. "Let me get dressed."

I understand that most people go to the door when visiting other people, but at that particular hour that wasn't an option for me, and not because we had some sort of secret tryst. Emma's roommate was a tyrant, and waking her would've spelled the end of me. It was a pity Emma had to live with her, but she had no choice. Emma hardly made anything working behind the desk at the truck dealership and she couldn't stay at home so long as her dad kept losing his temper. The roommate was a friend of a friend and let her stay there for groceries, provided she was quiet. I wanted to get a decent job and move her in with me but I couldn't keep my head focused long enough to stay in one place. What I really wanted was for her to be able to go to school. She's two years younger than I am but she would say things sometimes that were so unexpected and right, I was sure she understood the world in a way I never could.

Emma slipped out of the house and quietly closed the door behind her. Her hair was down, and she was still blinking the sleep out of her eyes. She was in jeans and a heavy gray sweatshirt with a red T-shirt hanging out the bottom. I knew the shirt; it read *Blue Ridge Gas and Heating*, and she wore it to bed a lot. I'd given it to her after I quit Blue Ridge Gas and Heating last winter.

"It's kind of chilly for April," she said.

"It's also before six o'clock."

"Is it? Jesus."

"I was at Staunton Donut. I missed you."

"You lost your job for a donut?"

She had a way of making so much sense it made me realize I didn't have any. What could I say? I toed the loose gravel in the driveway. I asked, "Want to go for a ride?"

We got into the car and pulled away. Soon enough the car was full of that burning smell old cars get when the heat comes on, and we were driving through Staunton with me remembering that the only place open was Staunton Donut and realizing I had nowhere to take her.

Staunton's a sensible town—not the most glamorous place in Virginia—but it does have a claim to fame: Our nation's twenty-eighth president, Woodrow Wilson, was born here. I can tell you everything you ever wanted to know about Woodrow Wilson because every single year between fourth and eighth grade I went on field trips to the house where he was born.

Emma and I were driving past the Staunton Correctional Facility for the second time when she asked where we were going and what the big idea was. I was getting nervous because I didn't have the answer to either of those questions, and that's when I noticed the light seeping up all around us. I knew if I made a U-turn I could get to Route 250 in a hurry.

"We're going to the mountains," I said. "I had to drive around first to get the timing right."

"Right for what?"

"Sunrise."

Emma darted her eyes out the window, as if expecting the sun to appear any second. She said, "Where'd you get that idea?"

"Nowhere. I'm being romantic."

"Are there roses in the backseat?"

"Only empty Coke cans."

"They're red," she said. "That's something."

The car choked, and Emma raised her eyebrows. The car was twelve years old, and everything about it was on the verge of ruin. Only one of the four windows still rolled down, and the two back doors wouldn't open. I had to put air in the tires twice a week, and the windshield wipers worked so poorly I'd taken them off. At various points during the winter, the car had simply refused to start. It wasn't insured, either.

I asked, "Were you sleeping okay when I came by?"

"Like a baby."

"Because I didn't want to interrupt a good dream if you were having one."

"I don't remember my dreams. It's too much work."

"Never?"

"Only the really good ones."

I tried to picture what Emma's good dreams must be like. I saw them as thoughtful events with the night so quiet you could hear meteors dropping and the universe stretching. I wanted to think I was there, but that's not how I pictured them. Instead I saw Emma alone, sitting on the side of a hill, her eyes open, and the air so cool all you wanted to do was breathe it in over and over again. She

was letting the wind move the grass over her feet, and she
was picking blue stars out of the sky.

"Are you mad at me?" I asked.

"No," she said. "I haven't seen the sunrise in years."

"What about the job?"

"That I worry about."

"You shouldn't."

"Why? Because you'll get another job?"

"Because I always do," I said. "I'm good at it. Not
keeping jobs, but finding them."

"I need a boyfriend who can *keep* a job," she said.
"Where can I find a guy like *that*?"

I said, "Charlottesville." I said it because every time I'd
been there I'd run into guys who looked like they could
hold jobs. It was true, even if it wasn't the answer she
wanted.

It occurred to me then that I didn't know where I was.
I recognized this as a serious problem. We were heading
west on 250, and I knew the sun rises in the east, but
250 isn't exactly a straight shot, and the east can seem
nonspecific when you're heading the opposite way, and
mountains are beginning to crowd all around you.

I tried to read the atmosphere for hints, but it was still
sort of dark, and the sky above the Allegheny Mountains
is hazy and smudged in the morning. I've worked a lot
of jobs, and plenty of them have started early, and I can
tell you that the way the earth wakes here is something.
The mountains start off as chalk lines in the sky, all shape,
and as the sun gets higher, the mountains begin to fill in
with color. On a clear day you can even make out trees,

the black borders that light draws around clusters of pine and oak. The whole world comes to life in the way that I imagine a painting must—general and then more and more specific. I'm no artist, but I think that artists probably paint that way because it's the way God makes the morning each day, and each of us wants to be as close to Him as we can.

Just past Churchville I got off the highway. Through a series of turns I navigated the car onto a small road that became less paved the farther we went. Without a doubt, it seemed like it led somewhere. Quietly, Emma looked impressed. I knew that for the first time all morning she trusted me, believed that the sun was going to rise, and that we were going to see it. She grabbed my right hand, and the tips of her fingers were cold. I pushed her fingers into a fist and covered her hand. I'd never been on this road before. The only reason I'd gotten off the highway was because I knew the sun shoots up quicker than you think, that it was shooting up soon, and we needed to be out of the car when it happened.

Emma said, "We've been going uphill for a while now."

"We're going to the top."

"What's there?"

"Clouds. Sky." In the immediate distance I saw a silver water tower, about forty feet tall. I added, "A water tower."

"Are we stopping for a drink? Are we giants?"

"We're going to watch the sunrise. Remember how it's beautiful? How romantic I am?"

The road began to level. There was a paved space near the base of the water tower, and I neatly steered the car into one of its four parking spots. We were at the top of a good-sized hill that you could've called a mountain. It must have looked like I knew what I was doing. We stepped out of the car, and I glanced at my watch as if checking to see if we'd made good time.

She said, "This view is beautiful."

"It's a good spot."

She reached her hand toward the horizon and said, "It's too bad the sun can't rise *here*."

I turned around. In the east, the Blue Ridge Mountains were barely visible. It was the mountains in front of us that were really breathtaking. I said, "We're in the wrong place."

"It's all right."

"We didn't go in far enough. We could've seen it rise over the Alleghenies. I took you to the wrong mountain."

"No. It's fine."

"Wow, the wrong mountain. That's great."

"It'll still be beautiful."

"There's a blanket in my trunk. We can sit down."

"Let's do that."

I went to my trunk. All I had inside were a spare tire and some empty grocery bags. I said, "I don't have a blanket."

"Sit with me anyway," she said. "The grass won't be that wet."

It really did seem cold for the middle of April. Maybe it was the hour, or the altitude, but I was shivering, and Emma was breathing in exaggerated breaths just to watch the air congeal and dissolve. I put my arm over her shoulder to bring her in closer. Emma's beauty came out strongest in the cold. Red settled in her cheeks, and her full build seemed healthier and more alive. Her sharp blue eyes were striking when the sky was white, when the earth turned glossy with ice.

She said, "It won't be long now. I can tell by the colors."

"I thought you hadn't seen the sunrise in years."

"You don't forget."

"Let's get out of here."

"Are you crazy? It's just starting. Look, I can see the top of the ball now."

I loved that she called the sun a *ball*. I said, "This isn't a good spot."

She looked at me incredulously. "Stop. Enjoy this with me."

"Let's climb to the top of the water tower. Let's watch it there."

Emma looked up at the water tower. It was only about twenty feet from where we were sitting. There was a chain fence that ran the perimeter of its base, and I figured we could get over it. The ladder leading to the top seemed sturdy enough. I wondered how many gallons of water the tower held, how the water got all the way to people's sinks and bathtubs. We seemed so far away from that.

"No," she said.

"Seriously," I said. "We'll climb straight to the top."

"I'll fall. I'm scared."

"I'll catch you."

"But you'll be at the top, too."

"Then I won't let you fall."

"Can we do that?" She'd grabbed my arm without

realizing it and was squeezing fairly hard. "Can we just climb a water tower?"

"I'm almost positive that we can."

"It will be your fault if I die."

Getting over the fence proved harder than I'd thought. There were no holes to poke your feet into, and the chain along the top had been stretched into spikes. Through some awkward maneuvering, I managed to heave myself over. As suspected, I found that the fence door could be opened from the inside without a key. I pushed it open and bowed respectfully at the waist. Emma said "*Merci beaucoup*" as she entered, her right hand absently waving in the invisible entourage that followed her.

I walked to the tower and put my ear against it, half-expecting to hear water sloshing around inside.

Emma said, "It's not a conch. This isn't the ocean."

I grabbed the rungs of the ladder with both hands. I climbed about five feet, gave the ladder a good shake, and then jumped backward onto the ground. The ladder was firm, steel, cold to the touch. I said, "You go first. I'll be right behind you."

"I'm trusting you," she said.

"Don't look down. Take one rung at a time."

"I love you, Mark." It wasn't something we said to each other very often. It was understood, and we said it mechanically from time to time, but it was nice to hear it then.

We were most of the way up the ladder when Emma stopped climbing. She said, "I'm not doing this anymore."

"You have to." I was two rungs below her. "Another ten feet is all."

"I think I'll stay here."

"Emma. The sunrise."

"This isn't fun." She looked back at me, and when I met her eyes, she reluctantly continued climbing. "I can't be falling off water towers."

"Wait until you see the view."

There was plenty of room to sit at the top. There was a small guardrail, and we kept our distance from it, sitting a few feet from the edge of the tower. I said, "They'd have to drain the whole tower if someone found us up here. Down to the last drop."

"Why's that?" she asked.

"Poison."

"Because they'd think we poisoned the supply?"

"Who knows? You can never be too careful." I put my hand on her back and kneaded at the knots that formed between her shoulders. "I mean, what business do we have being up here?"

"Now you say these things."

"I'm just saying it doesn't look too good."

"Maybe they'd think we were watching the sunrise."

"That I was trying to be romantic."

"You still are, right?"

"Yes," I said. "But it would be better if we could see the sun."

The sun was becoming increasingly obscured by clouds as it moved over the Blue Ridge. It was a mostly foggy morning. Nothing unusual. Something I should have anticipated, really.

I said, "This is a poor performance."

"It's not so bad."

"It didn't seem as foggy in Staunton."

"What would you do if I started to cry?"

I turned to her. She had full, clear tears building in her eyes. When she blinked, the tears slid down her cheeks and off her face. Her eyelashes were bright black.

"Emma. What's wrong?"

"Nothing."

"You're crying," I said.

"I know." She laughed. She stretched her legs and drew them back in. "I don't know why."

"Jesus."

"I'm not sad. Really, I swear."

"You've got me fooled."

"I'm not, Mark. You have to believe me. I'm not sad. I don't know why I'm crying. This has never happened before."

A crow landed on the guardrail and eyed Emma and me with suspicion. I stared at it until it flew away.

"It is beautiful," she said.

"It's a bit of a disaster," I said. "How long did we see the sun for? A minute? Two minutes?"

"No," she said. "No, no, no."

"Emma?"

"Being here with you. I don't know." She was still crying. It was a funny thing—she gave me this small, soft look, and I started crying, too.

"Oh, perfect," I said.

"Maybe it's the altitude."

"Or the water. There is a lot of water here."

"A couple of winners we are," she said.

"A real mess."

The crow returned with other crows. They assembled along the guardrail with a dark, serious formality.

"We have an audience," Emma said.

"It's morning," I said. "You can't really tell, but the sun's up now, behind the clouds."

"It comes quick once it gets going."

Emma dropped her head onto my shoulder. I pushed her hair behind her ears and rested my hand on the back of her neck. That morning, I had no way of knowing that she was already two weeks pregnant, that the next month she would turn to me over dinner and say, Mark, I'm late. I had no way to know that she would insist on having the baby, that I would nod my head slowly and continue to wander through jobs, saving money here and there as I went. I couldn't know then that when Stephen was born my whole ribcage would seem to tighten. That I could hold, inside me, something too large for my own body: an awe I would never be able to detach from fear. That I could love Emma in a way so different it was as if we were each someone else. What would I have even believed when we'd been so grateful for the heat of the sun on a morning that had been a little cooler than most?

The crows stepped off the tower, and I watched them until they folded into the white of the clouds. Emma and I slid to the edge of the tower. All the birds were gone, and below us the earth was reddening, hardening to meet its midday form. Emma said something about the clay, or maybe it was the sky, and like that we were crawling down the ladder, our legs moving faster than our arms. We ran to the car. At first it wouldn't start, and Emma looked worried, but soon enough it did, and we were flying down the hill, the land around us dressing frantically into blues and greens for morning.

She asked, "Where do you want to go?"

I said, "Charleston."

"In West Virginia? Why?"

"For breakfast. I know a place that makes unbelievable omelets."

"I hate eggs."

"But you're going to love Charleston."

Emma pushed her hands against the dashboard. Before us, the mountains seemed like things we could take in our hands and weigh. I knew that Charleston was as good a place as anywhere else in the world to be right then, and I figured we had enough gas in the car to get there.

I KNOW WHO YOU ARE

I was sitting at a desk in New York, an enormous desk
with too many small things on it. The smallest thing was
a paperclip. I mauled the paperclip. It was the only one.
I turned it into an S and then a triangle. With my index
finger, I launched the triangle into the door. The paperclip
bounced cleanly onto the carpet.

I picked up the phone when it rang, and the voice
roared into my right ear. I said, What do you want? What
do you want? I said this five, six, seven times, and then I
hung up the phone. It didn't ring again, which made me
irrationally proud. This ended up depressing me. Nervously,
I looked for something to pick up and then drop. I picked
up an empty coffee mug, but it felt too light.

This wasn't my desk. This wasn't even my building.

The enormous window confirmed what I'd expected:
I was too high in the air. The people looked like different
colored candies. The cars looked like crude plastic toys.
Other buildings blocked the sky, and the blinds were
wide open. Briefly, I considered hiding beneath the table.
I opened all of the drawers. They were filled with thick
papers. They looked unread. I began to read them.

He was in a lot of trouble. He had seen things. Had
he named names? It was a distinct possibility. Reading the
papers, I grew worried for his future. I didn't want to see him
in trouble. I'd grown, reading his personal correspondence,
to care for his concerns. I'd come to see them as my own.
I picked up the phone and requested a BLT and bottle of
Irish whiskey. The secretary asked who I was, so I made the
request again, and she said, Okay, fine, you got it. I didn't wait
for her to arrive. I cleared the desk of the too many small
things. Confronted only with his desk, I was able to clear my
mind. It wasn't long before I'd filled a thick paper of my own.
I didn't wait for the secretary's approval. I folded the paper
the delicate way you fold something destined for an envelope.
I placed the paper in my left breast pocket and left the room.

Then I was sprinting through the hallways. Everybody
noticed. I paused at a door that demanded some sort
of code. I punched numbers indiscriminately. The door
shrieked in protest. I moved to another door with another
mystery box. I attacked it.

A woman approached me. She was dressed like an
angel. Her wings fluttered faintly beneath her white jacket.
I had to suppress an overwhelming temptation to touch
her tightly-coiled hair.

"You want that door." She pointed across the enormous room. "That's the door you came in."

I averted my eyes.

"It's easy to be confused." The angel reached for my shoulder but found my chest.

Her hand was too warm. I moved to the door, not because she told me to, but to keep moving. I moved through the door and into the long hallway, where I burst into a full sprint. I ran past the elevator and down the stairs. I couldn't breathe. I leaned into the railing. For as far as I could see, there was concrete. Above me, below me. There wasn't one window. It occurred to me that I could be anywhere. A door opened. I had no idea where the door was.

The angel was extending her hand. I was meeting it. She was giving me back my bag, and I was slinging it over my shoulder, avoiding her eyes completely, which wasn't working. She only wanted to help.

"They really are the best sandwiches," she said. "If I had it my way, we'd have them every day. I don't know why we don't."

"They're sort of expensive," I lied.

"Not that expensive!" She laughed. "Not for how good they are, I mean."

"The best."

She nodded. How little she understood me. I had to resist the temptation to grab her by the shoulders and explain everything. I could help her. I considered starting the tutorial but I was having difficulty breathing. I put my hands on my knees. I tried not to think about how it looked because what does that matter?

"I ought to go." She sort of tapped the sandwich bag, even though it was under my arm.

"The best," I said.

She attempted to smile.

The street was full of people. I shouldered into every suit. I looked so innocent plowing through the crowd. I didn't mean to make eye contact. His eyes were dry with violence. Only occasionally did he snap his lids shut. I resisted the urge to look away, submitting to the equally powerful urge to hold his stare. This satisfied the man. It wasn't deliberately that I began to follow him after he dismissed me.

Here the crowd served me well. I maneuvered deftly among the brisk-moving gray slacks. I slipped in and out of storefronts so gently. I could have removed a man's watch and put it on my own wrist without the man so much as turning his head. People did turn their heads but not to notice me. Mostly, they focused on their own private urgencies. Maybe they acknowledged a persistent horn. Maybe they lingered on a child grabbing so desperately at an errant shirtsleeve there seemed something sinister in the woman's inattention. I understood her. I would have let the child grab too.

The man was no faster than anyone else. He followed the rhythms of the street like everyone. Like I did, in my private way. I slinked around lampposts and paused in doorways. When I drew too close, I found a phone booth. I flipped through the yellow pages, which hadn't been updated in years, which were filled with preposterous drawings. The anatomies were unenviable.

It wasn't long before he led me down a side street, darker than the others. I thought the lights were broken before realizing there were no lights. They weren't supposed to be necessary. I stared into a window and tried to make sense of the neon shapes. I couldn't tell what they were selling. I suspected beer or possibly fish. Every window pulsed with strange color. The man didn't pause. He'd seen this before. It was nothing to him to walk down a street on fire. There were fewer people on this street. They were all Asian, except for me. Except for the man. He moved leisurely down this street. There was something newly contemplative in his step. There were questions I wanted to ask him, like what did he mean looking at me that way. I didn't expect him to answer. I understood that he would soon lose me in a crowd or perhaps discover me. Despite understanding these things, I persisted, though my pace slowed.

We ended at an apartment far uptown. He carried a black umbrella, though it hadn't rained in weeks. The man paused at the door, as if trying to remember something essential he'd forgotten. I had the irrational fear he'd turn around and walk the several dozen blocks I'd followed him. He did not. He walked through one heavy door and then another. Both closed noisily. I hurried up the concrete steps and pushed on the door, hoping the lock hadn't caught. It had. I took a single step back. I sat on the steps, waiting for the man to come back or for someone else to let me in. I didn't expect to hear a window open, softly, as if to emphasize the man's control of the situation. That he could speak never occurred to me.

"I know who you are" is all he said.

What did he mean? That he knew I'd trailed him or that he'd seen me somewhere else? Worse, that he saw in me something he saw in himself, something he resented. It wasn't hard to understand. I shouted that I knew him too, but the window was closed—even his shadow gone—and I didn't know him, not at all.

It was a forgotten part of the city, absent subway stops or even post office boxes. I retraced my steps. I still had a delivery to make, though the sandwiches were cold. I began to eat one. They really were good sandwiches. I left the lettuce on the street. I needed to speak to the enormous Mexican who made them. His English was better than my Spanish. I didn't speak any Spanish, and he didn't speak any English. I didn't know what to do between deliveries but cut tomatoes. There was no end to the tomatoes we cut in the backroom. Occasionally, I smoked because that's what Ramon did when he wasn't cutting. He smoked an obscure brand that burned away as soon as you lit the paper. He bit off the filters, possibly swallowing them. I wondered what he'd think about my mission, which was how I'd come to think about following the man who knew me. Probably, Ramon would exhale thoughtfully. This was his answer to most things.

The street was even darker now. I had no sense of the time. A dog trotted unconcerned down the center of the street, a flyer firm in its jaw. The flyer was still in the blue plastic bag. Idiotically, I wondered what the paper was selling. I suspected products for hair loss. I was losing almost all of mine, unruly strands and then actual piles on the bathtub's unforgiving white. Increasingly, my wish to go gray before bald seemed an impossibility. I was thirty years old. The dog looked about ten. There was plenty of gray around its muzzle. The dog was walking toward me, and I was walking toward the dog. I didn't know where all the cars were. Possibly, nobody could afford them. The dog was fearless; if anything, the dog sensed my fear. The dog had seen worse than a skinny man with a large bag. I threw one of the sandwiches before the dog, but it didn't halt its trot or even drop the newspaper, which drooped out of the animal's jaw like an enormous forgotten cigarette. Ramon would know what to do with the dog. He'd handle it with the casual brutality I'd seen him employ on the mangy strays that scratched against the back door. I'd pitied them before but I wouldn't next time.

I backed against a storefront, where I reasoned the dog might not follow me. It raised its aging snout toward me before walking coldly by. Who was this animal to take such an exalted position? I considered chasing it down the street, but it turned blithely at a green light, and I never saw the dog again. I crept from door to door. Somebody asked me later if I was on drugs, like I couldn't just be alone with my trembling thoughts.

My apartment was above train tracks. People think of the subway as being underground, but that's not always the way it works. Late at night, I'd sit on my living room couch and stare through the kitchen window at the approaching yellow. The living room and kitchen were more or less the same thing. I didn't have a television or even a lamp. When night came, I relied entirely on other people's light. That might seem an obstinate way to live, but it suited me.

I didn't have a lot of visitors. The cabinets were mostly empty, as was the refrigerator. Sometimes when I coaxed a stranger upstairs—my apartment was a fifth-floor walkup—I put out a plate of cheese and crackers. Sometimes I had to scrape off a little mold, and usually the crackers were stale, but I could be counted on to provide these two things, though nobody counted on me for anything. I ate a stale cracker. I watched a train approach. I waved to the people on the train, though there was no way for them to see me. More than once, I'd searched my dark apartment from the moving train—imagining my own loneliness—but the angles were such that you couldn't see anything. Still, I waved.

I reviewed the face. I hadn't gotten a good look, though I knew it was angry. I was angry too, but this was hard to justify. Anyone observing impartially would finger me as the offender, and I didn't disagree with this judgment. The first question anyone would ask: Why did I follow him? Naturally, I could summon reasons, but I wasn't thinking about them as I moved through the streets. I was thinking about how I needed to help the angel. I was thinking about the man whose files I'd read, how much trouble he was in, if there was any way to avoid violence. These thoughts were unconscious; I only understood them when I returned to the apartment. I had no conscious thoughts I could remember, except that the man I'd followed understood me. I worried that he was in love with the angel. That he was coming after the man I was trying to help. That, above all, he understood my fear. I took out a sheet of paper, though I could barely see in the dark. I didn't know how to address him.

I pointed out that he, more than most, should understand where I was coming from. What I was trying to do. Surely, he understood why I'd followed him. That didn't warrant discussion. What mattered was what happened next. On this point, I waited for the next train. I waited a long time, owing to the hour, which was late or perhaps early. I suggested we meet in Bennett Park, based on a sign I'd passed. It seemed, in that moment, a discreet place. I didn't offer a reason for meeting or imply that there ought to be one, a gesture—or lack thereof—that satisfied me completely.

Next I considered how to deliver the letter, which I folded the delicate way you fold something destined for an envelope. Only in reaching for my left breast pocket did I discover the other letter, which I placed on the table. I examined this letter as if someone had handed it to me then, as if I had nothing to do with its composition. I considered the two letters the way one weighs rival tomatoes in a market. I only needed one. Shaking with excitement, I placed one letter in my left pocket and one in my right, deciding I would decide later.

I startled myself awake in the middle of the night. Possibility pulsed through my veins. I began to weigh the virtues of each letter. Unconsciously, I reached for them, but they were still in my jacket. I stumbled from my bed to the solitary chair in the kitchen, where the jacket stood sentinel. I rifled through the pockets and clung to the letters. In darkness, they bore no resemblance to anything I'd encountered. I was unable to return to sleep.

At dawn, I made my way to work. The restaurant didn't open until eight, but sandwiches were constructed well before then. Ramon was already there. No matter how early I arrived, Ramon was already at work. I wasn't certain he had a home. I didn't have the courage to ask.

"*Qué pasa?*" I said.

He waved his knife past a mountain of tomatoes in the corner. I got to work.

"There's something I have to ask you," I said. "I need some advice. Don't feel pressured to tell me what I want to hear. I have two letters. I don't really want to get into what the letters are about because that's not what matters. Well, it *matters*. But it's not the primary thing."

Ramon applied pesto before depositing a single slice of Swiss. He was famous for his stinginess with the Swiss.

"I need to choose. I can't go around carrying both. What kind of madman goes around carrying two letters? Here's where you enter. Here's where your input is welcome. Do I deliver the first letter or the second?" I was doing a sloppy job with the tomatoes. "I can handle your honest opinion. Don't hold back."

Did Ramon pause before putting down the pesto? Certainly, he didn't say anything, not in English or Spanish. He wrapped the sandwich in one fluid gesture and moved to the next. He had a lot of sandwiches to make before the front doors opened. Nobody else was making them, or even helping. I didn't take his silence personally. I finished the prep work and poured myself a coffee from the enormous black thermos. I didn't want to drink it—caffeine makes me nervous—I just wanted the heat on my hands. The steam opened my eyes.

Somebody had parked the truck wrong. It wasn't difficult to park the truck right if you cared, but nobody cared. I jammed myself into the driver's seat and started the engine. I climbed into the back, where there were no sandwiches. That was my job, loading the sandwiches. I turned on the radio. A bunch of noise about contests, about what number caller. It was hard to muster support. I'd called once, but nobody picked up, which I thought was rude. After five minutes, I grew worried I was being charged. Thirty seconds later there was a winner. Her voice was full of youth and, already, money.

I left the truck running. There was no heat in the truck, so some enterprising maniac had torn off the panel between your legs and the engine. It's hard to describe. But you could see more than wires. You could see actual engine parts and you could feel fire. Some days it seemed my shoes would burst into flames, though my fingers, even in gloves, couldn't move. This was the bad winter. This was the winter a hundred ambulances got stuck in the snow. I had the gloves with the fingertips exposed, so you could smoke, though I only smoked with Ramon. Those were just the gloves I had. You could make them look like a terrible accident had occurred, which was funny because one had. Not funny, exactly, but someone did lose a finger on the meat slicer or at least the tip of one. The doctor sewed the tip back on. Imagine! The doctor sewed the tip back onto the finger, and the fingernail started growing again. Medicine.

The truck was old, white, enormous. It didn't want
to be started. I was sympathetic. I left the truck running
for a long time before I made it leave the store with two-
hundred-and-sixty-seven sandwiches. I didn't have to
count them. If Ramon wrote *267*, that was the number.

The streets were empty this early. Trash was the only
thing moving, and even an errant wrapper floated without
urgency. Snow was black to the point where it no longer
resembled snow so much as dirt. There were huge holes
in the street, and the tires found each of them. There were
no shocks in the truck that made any kind of difference,
so I felt it all. Still, there was a luxury to driving among
all these buildings. Every time, I felt like I was getting
away with something, even when I was just doing my job,
delivering sandwiches to hungry offices.

I steered toward the office of the man I was trying to
help. I assumed he wouldn't be coming into work today or
possibly ever again. I pulled up to a meter. At this hour,
it didn't require payment. I turned off the engine and
considered my options.

The doorman pretended to know me. He wasn't the
only one. They look out for us. They assume we are who we
say we are. I was alone in the elevator bank, which gave me
more time. I didn't take it to the top. Nobody remembered
me, despite my running. I wasn't even in disguise. I asked
where they wanted the sandwiches, but nobody answered.
I headed for the office of the man I was trying to help. Just
from looking at the door, I could see that it was locked.
I tried the door anyhow. I took the sandwich bag off my
shoulder. Lightly, I knocked.

The man who answered didn't look like he had a lot of time. He opened the door looking like he was expecting a secretary. He didn't have kind words for her. I picked up my bag and entered the office. He closed the door behind us. He didn't have to show me the chair. I had my hand in my pocket on the letter. He sat behind the desk and folded his hands over a black pen. It was the only thing on the desk and then it was gone.

"You're probably wondering what I'm doing in your office." I kept my eyes on the missing black pen. "You're probably thinking, Who is this delivery guy sitting in my office and what does he think he knows?"

The man didn't look like he was thinking this, but he was content to let me talk before having me thrown out of the building.

"I'll keep it short." I gripped the letter. "I know about your problems. We don't need to get into why. I'm not the only one."

When the man raised his hand, the pen was gone. It was in his other hand. Was he taking notes?

"Here's what I think. You have options. It might seem like you don't, but you do." I waited for him to ask about his options, but he remained silent. "I wrote you a letter."

The man lowered the pen and picked up the phone. The phone I'd used to order the BLT and whiskey that never arrived. The man pressed a few buttons. He waited, and I grew frantic over the terrible thing that would surely happen next.

"Okay, I get it." When I stood, my legs were shaking. "I don't have to read it. I can show myself the door."

Walking to the door was harder than I'd anticipated. My legs didn't do the things they were supposed to do. I had to pause at the desk. I had to rest my weight for a moment. The man watched me. He had one hand on the phone and the other hand on the pen. It occurred to me that the door was locked. That the blinds were closed. That nobody could see anything, and this was how he wanted it.

"Sit down," the man said. "Whatever you think you know is wrong. You don't know anything, so let's start there."

I took the letter out of my pocket. I folded it into fours and placed it beside my wallet. I sat and, cautiously, I listened.

"I'm going to give you fifteen seconds to explain yourself. You have ten seconds. You would be smart to start talking."

I opened my mouth, but my tongue didn't do the thing it was supposed to do. My tongue stalled at the roof of my mouth. The man offered no pity. His tongue did whatever he told it to do. He had no problems with his words. He used them sparingly.

"You really do have problems," I said.

"Everyone has problems. You have problems."

"I know I do."

"You have no idea."

"I have, I think, a fairly good idea."

The man opened the drawer where I'd uncovered his problems. He removed several hundred papers and spread them across the desk. The man filled his desk with papers and waited for me to say something.

"I know about those," I said.

"You know about too many things."

"That sounds ominous. Like maybe it's from a movie."

"It doesn't sound like anything. It's a fact. We're on the twenty-third floor. That's another fact."

"I understand what you mean."

"You have no idea."

The man wasn't amused. He wasn't having a good time. But I was lying, and he was wrong. He wasn't getting rid of me until I told him what he wanted to hear. I didn't know what that might be, so I made up something. I don't know what part of my brain it came from. I was sitting in his office, and he wanted something, so I gave it to him. The world doesn't have to be complicated.

He leaned back in his chair. He looked disappointed that papers were still on the desk. The phone annoyed him in its silence. The light coming in from the window annoyed him in its lightness. The world annoyed me too. I said something about this, but he wasn't listening, and I didn't repeat myself.

"Okay, okay, okay, okay, okay," he finally said.

I didn't understand.

"You should leave," he said. "I thought it was something else. I thought you were someone else."

"But I can help."

He was already standing. He was already opening the door, and I was walking through it, my bag slung clumsily over my shoulder. Nobody was waiting for us. Nobody even knew we were there. Neither of us understood what happened next. I reached into my bag and removed our most popular sandwich. He recognized it. He unwrapped the sandwich and begin to eat it, half in the office, half in the hallway. He ate very neatly, difficult for this sandwich, which was mostly barbecue sauce. I envied his control. Neither of us said anything. I pulled out the same kind of sandwich, and it was delicious.

"Can we talk about this?" I asked between bites. "Do we have options?"

He made polite chewing noises. In the office, the phone would not stop ringing.

"I'm not judging," I said. "God knows."

He pointed to the long hallway. It was even longer than I'd remembered. He didn't stop pointing until I started moving. There were no angels. There were men hunched over keyboards filled with crumbs and women talking to other women between gray partitions. Tacked to the partitions were pictures, comics, calendars, inspirational quotes, deadlines, reminders, report cards. Nobody got less than a B+.

I must have been gone a long time. The truck had an orange traffic ticket. It had two tickets, maybe three, and the doorman shrugged. He didn't seem concerned, which I didn't appreciate. He could see how upset I was. He said, The thing is, but he didn't have anything to add, not one thing.

I felt bad for Ramon. The sandwiches were going bad. The sandwiches in my bag and the sandwiches in the truck. It was raining or maybe snowing. Through some combination of the two, I drove uptown. The roads were coated in black

ice. Cars threatened to drift into each other at every light.
Some succeeded. Men leapt out of the cars, their arms
already waving. I waved along to music. The truck had two
door speakers, both broken. It was my fault. I tapped with
too much spirit. I kicked everything I could reach. The
speaker on the passenger side door was someone else's fault,
possibly the guy who ripped off the paneling. Really, the
truck had a lot of problems. It didn't require keys, either.

People were driving too fast. They sped past me en
route to important errands and meetings they couldn't
miss. My task was less urgent. I knew I'd be fired. I'd had
enough chances. I had two thousand dollars worth of
undeliverable sandwiches. Plus gas and labor. Plus the
truck, which I might not return. I hadn't decided. There
was a sweater on the passenger seat. There was a flashlight
with batteries and maybe three dollars in change. I didn't
care for the sweater. I folded the traffic tickets into the
sweater and fed them to the engine. I had to crack the
window when the smoke grew too thick.

Soon I was in front of the apartment. I unbuckled my
seat belt and turned off the engine. I ate another sandwich.
It was not as delicious. Nobody left or entered the building.
Not even a postman. I began to suspect that the man I was
following was the only person who lived here. I wondered
if he owned or rented. It was so expensive in the city,
even in a rundown neighborhood. Even in an abandoned
building. I couldn't see his window from the truck, which
complicated things.

I stepped out of the truck, and there he was, watching
me. I considered waving. He lit a pipe. I hadn't pictured

him as a pipe user. It made me rethink some things. Like what was I doing here? At least, that's what I wanted to think. Truthfully, I didn't rethink anything. I nearly waved, but he was already closing the window without so much as putting out his pipe. The blinds were down, and he was a shadow. His smoke was a shadow. I felt so alone.

Slowly, the building's front door opened. The man let the door close behind him before acknowledging me. He motioned for me to approach, and I felt nervous. I felt like maybe it was time to get back in the truck and pretend I hadn't twice stood outside his window, waiting for him to do what he was doing now, which was extend his hand as though we really were friends. As though there was nothing strange about the situation. I considered putting the letter in his hand, but we hadn't talked about that yet. We hadn't talked about anything. I'd followed him, and he'd let himself be followed, though I was more aware of this than he. It was hard to know what he was thinking. He still wasn't speaking. The only thing he'd ever said was, I know who you are, and true to his words, he remembered me. His handshake hurt. His eyes were as violent as I'd remembered and very open.

"I have a letter," I said. "You don't have to read it. Maybe it's better if—"

"You came, at great expense, to deliver a letter?"

I didn't know how to answer that question. He was as patient as the other man was impatient. There was no reason why they should be the same.

"I did," I decided.

He didn't feel compelled to add anything, which I

thought was reasonable. I produced the letter, which he didn't acknowledge. His eyes were fixed on me, though he showed no actual curiosity as to why I was here. More like disgust. More like anger. He fussed with his pipe. I wished I had one. Anything but the letter, really.

"Maybe I made a mistake," I said. "I thought it was something else. I thought you were someone else."

The man smoked thoughtfully. He was in no hurry. The tobacco was more floral than I'd expected, though it didn't smell like flowers. It smelled like a sunny pasture of smoke. I had an overwhelming temptation to try this pipe. I nearly asked before turning to the truck.

"You didn't come just to leave." The man sounded like he was enjoying himself now. But it wasn't a question. He didn't care about me, except to mock me. He didn't care about why I was here.

I didn't pause at the door. I turned the keys and I was on my way. In the rearview mirror, I watched him get smaller before disappearing completely.

The West Side Highway is hard to get onto but easy once you're there. I worked my way to the far left lane. The traffic wasn't as aggressive as I'd imagined. I felt in place and at peace. I wouldn't really be fired. So the sandwiches wouldn't be delivered on time or possibly at all. Ramon would know what to do. I considered calling him but I didn't have a phone and didn't speak Spanish and Ramon didn't answer the phone, anyhow.

I came to a long traffic light. It's always a surprise to find lights on the highway. Is it really a highway if it has lights? Sometimes the lights take much longer than ninety

seconds. Sometimes the lights take ten, fifteen minutes.
Sometimes you have to just *run* the lights because, really,
they're never going to change. I looked around to see if
anyone was considering doing this. I was willing to follow
his lead. Or her lead. But probably his. I had things to
tell people! Frantically, I reached for the letters, but they
were gone. Had I dropped them in my rush to leave? I
flirted with the possibility of the man having stolen them,
but it was a preposterous idea. He'd listened to me only
to increase his amusement. The other man was no better,
just more paranoid. The light would never be green. It was
something I was going to have to deal with, somehow.

Of course, I could write more letters. I had a limitless
supply of information to draw from. The next letters
would be more insightful. I was beginning to be glad I'd
lost the two. Perhaps I hadn't lost them at all. Perhaps I'd
jettisoned them, knowing I was capable of better. Sitting at
the light, I was already drafting the first words of the next
letter. I didn't even require paper. The car to my right crept
forward, though the light was still red. I moved forward
too, but the driver ignored me. He had somewhere to be,
something important to find. I could help.

It wasn't reasonable to expect recognition at once. I
had to be patient. People need time to work through their
preconceptions. People want you to earn your success. It
isn't unfair. I had to show them exactly what I could do,
given the chance. How I could help. How I already had.
Eventually, people would look at me and say, I know who
you are. Just saying it would make them happy. And their
happiness would make me happy.

PURITAN HOTEL, BARNSTABLE

When Michael and Elaine arrived at Cape Cod Hospital, Michael didn't know there was a tumor the size of a ping-pong ball in his brother's head. His brother had said it was nothing too serious, and Michael was surprised to see Connor's head completely shaven, to find he'd lost nearly ten pounds. Before Michael could say anything, Connor pointed to his temple and relayed the facts that Doctor Saramago had given him. The tumor needed to be removed, and the procedure could be dangerous.

Michael put his hand on the edge of Connor's bed. "How did you get so skinny?" he asked.

"They don't feed me here," Connor said. "My insurance won't cover it."

"You look like you're from the future with that haircut."

Connor put his hand on his head and shook it. "Outlook hazy. Try again later."

Michael looked at Elaine, who was standing along the back wall of the room. Her face was turned toward the door, as though, out of politeness, she hadn't been listening. They'd been together for two years, but this was the first time they'd gone to Barnstable. She said little on the drive down from Boston, and when they were in the elevator on the way to the third floor, she offered to wait outside.

"Can you feel it?" Michael asked.

"It feels like calculus."

"Jesus, Connor. Why didn't you tell me?"

"I'm twenty-five years old." He pushed the sheets off his chest, revealing a thin blue gown. Michael watched Connor's chest rise when he inhaled. "I still can't believe it."

"Who knows?"

"Dad doesn't know."

Michael rubbed his hand along the sheets to see where Connor's legs were before he sat. He tried to imagine having a ping-pong ball in his head. There are, he knew, all sorts of shocking things about the human body. Is it the small intestine that's thirty feet long? But this was different. Tumors aren't organs or bones. As a child, he'd owned a book on Louis Pasteur that showed the rabies vaccine as a line of French soldiers and the rabies as menacing, oversized bugs. It was clear that the bugs had little business inside the sick boy's body, and the soldiers bayoneted them heroically.

"Here's what I'm thinking," Michael said. "I'm thinking

we're going to get you through this."

"I'm high as a kite. I should tell you that."

"I thought they might have you on something."

"Tranquilizers. I begged for them, thinking they'd be stingy, but they handed them right over."

"When is the surgery?"

"Two days. It was supposed to be this afternoon."

Michael looked at his watch; he had a habit of doing that when anyone mentioned an important date or time. His office found it funny, and he knew it seemed affected, but the motion had become so instinctual he could rarely stop himself. Michael looked up and for the first time took in the room's sparseness. There were no other beds, and only rosary beads and a book—*Yaz: Baseball, the Wall, and Me*—lay on the bedside table. The window curtains were pulled open, but the winter sky was so gray it darkened the room's fluorescent lighting. None of the technology Michael associated with hospitals—heart monitors, electronically adjustable beds, a television bolted to the ceiling—was in the room. It didn't seem like a room to die in, but it didn't seem like a room to live in, either.

"Where's the closest hotel?" Michael asked. "We'll stay there."

Connor sat up in the bed. "You visited. That's enough. There's no reason to stay."

"We'd like to stay," Elaine said. "You shouldn't be alone."

"I'm used to being alone."

Michael waited for Connor to say something about Elaine's husband, but he didn't. He sighed and gathered the sheets around his neck. Elaine leaned forward and touched the sheets where his feet pushed up.

"You shouldn't be alone," she repeated.

Michael had forgotten how few hotels stay open past Labor Day. He assumed they would settle on one of the plainer motels off 28, but after an hour driving around town, he had to pull up to a parking lot payphone to search the yellow pages. His phone didn't get reception here. The hotel he found wasn't far from the hospital, which made sense, but annoyed him in a way that felt petty and selfish.

Michael and Elaine had packed a bag with a change of clothes in case they decided to stay the night. It was a precaution against fatigue more than anything else. When Connor called Michael the night before, Connor sounded annoyed but not worried. Just something that needs to come out, was the way he put it. Michael pressed further, and when Connor became defensive, Michael dropped it, saying only that he and Elaine would come down the next morning. Connor agreed begrudgingly, though it was clear to Michael that this was why Connor had called in the first place.

In the hotel room, Michael watched Elaine lay out their clean clothes on the bed. Michael was standing beside the heater beneath the window. He turned the heat to high, and warm blasts of air crashed around his chin and ears.

"You're surprised," she said.

"Of course I am." Michael thumbed the window curtain, which was thick and shabby.

"I had a feeling. Last night, I mean. When he called."

"I figured it was his appendix, something like that. I figured he was embarrassed by the whole thing."

"You should talk to him."

"We're not big talkers. We're not—" Michael searched for the right word. He was feeling defensive now, and he wanted to be as precise as possible. "We're not close like that."

He turned to the window. There were only a few cars in the parking lot, and he wondered how many of the people were here because of the hospital. It was too soon for something like this to happen, and he couldn't lose the feeling that it should be him there, if only because he was older. In CCD growing up, he told Father Murphy that he would sacrifice his life to save his brother's. The priests were always asking impossible questions so as to gauge the children's character, and Michael assumed this was the correct answer. His reason, and it seemed perfectly logical, was that his younger brother had more life left. Father Murphy nodded skeptically, and Michael thought of his face now as he saw his own reflection in the glass.

"I think you should go by yourself tomorrow," Elaine said.

"I want you there."

"You want me there, but Connor needs to talk to you. He can't talk to you the same with me there."

There was a chain link fence on the perimeter of the parking lot, and beyond the fence, a creek surrounded by trees. A few boys were smoking cigarettes along the edge of the creek, and Michael watched them, wondering where they had come from and what was on the other side of the trees. The boys lit new cigarettes from the tips of their old ones and dismissively threw the butts into the water.

"He might die." Michael didn't move his eyes from the window.

"What a thing to say."

"That's a possibility, though."

"Listen." Elaine's hands were on the sides of his abdomen. She pushed her face into the back of his neck. She didn't say anything else.

"I registered us under my name at the desk. I wasn't going to but then I did."

"I wish you hadn't done that."

Michael turned around so that he was facing her. "They gave me the sheet, and I just wrote it that way."

The next day, Connor was restless and alert. The tranquilizers, it seemed, had been abandoned.

"Can you believe these doctors? Now they say Tuesday." Connor crossed his arms morosely. "It would be one thing if my nurses were beautiful."

"They're pushing back your date to be as careful as possible." Michael had no idea whether or not this was true.

Connor eyed Michael suspiciously. "Did you bring me flowers?"

"I brought you a cheeseburger." Michael held up the grease-stained bag. "You need to eat something."

"I can't keep anything down. I'm too nervous. I haven't eaten a thing since I found out."

"Do you want to talk about it?"

"Oh, Jesus."

"What?"

"Did Elaine put you up to this? Are we supposed to have some big powwow?"

"I'm just worried about you."

"I'm worried about me, too. What do you want? I was having these headaches, and they wouldn't stop. The doctors ran some tests and then they told me it was a tumor. It wasn't the first thing I would have guessed. I shaved my head myself. Easier that way."

Michael put the bag on the bedside table. There was a vase with yellow roses there, and he tried to spot a tag without being obvious.

"Your girlfriend send these?" Michael fingered one of the roses.

"My girlfriend of five weeks." Connor scratched the back of his head. The gesture was more pronounced without his hair. "I wouldn't want to be in her shoes, either."

Michael nodded, trying to seem understanding without allowing her too much sympathy.

"Did Elaine leave already?"

"She's at the hotel. She thought we should be alone."

Connor reached over to take the bag. He peered into it skeptically, then put it back on the table. "Did her divorce go through yet?"

"He's not making it easy."

Connor stretched his arms and cracked his knuckles. It seemed like the movement of a healthy person, and Michael was glad to see it. "You know what I think," Connor said.

"They've been separated for three years."

"You won't be able to marry in the Church." To emphasize the tragedy of this, he repeated himself. "You won't."

Michael didn't want to get into it again and he didn't want to seem upset. He went to the corner of the room and dragged a chair to the foot of Connor's bed. Here, he was forced to look at his brother straight on, which was something he'd avoided. Connor's face was thinner, and with the bald head he seemed vaguely sinister, like a comic book villain. But he'd always been lean, and off the tranquilizers, his eyes were quick and his speech confident. There was an authority in the way he moved his legs beneath the sheets, as if to remind Michael that there were things he couldn't see.

"Have you been praying?" Michael asked.

"It hasn't made the tumor any smaller," Connor said. "But it's helped."

Connor absently picked up the rosary beads and rubbed one between his thumb and forefinger. It didn't look like he was praying. Michael didn't know what he was doing. After a few seconds, Connor placed the beads back on the table, beside the flowers.

"I was thinking," Connor began. "I have lots of time to do that lately."

Michael leaned forward to show that he was listening.

"Do you remember Paula Daltrey? We went to high school with her."

"Paula? Sure." The name sounded familiar.

"Well, I was thinking about her. She was very beautiful."

"Unlike the nurses." Michael waited until Connor

smiled before he did, too.

"We went ice skating once. Did you know that?"

"I don't think so."

"On the cranberry bog where we used to play hockey."

After harvest was over each October, the bog was flooded to protect the berries from frost. The bog froze over better than any of the ponds or rivers nearby, which were too brackish to skate on safely, and he and Connor and some other boys would play after school until the sky became a dimness they couldn't navigate through. There were no nets, and there was always a boy who didn't have skates, who promised he could play without them. That was, what, ten years ago? Twelve? Even at twenty-seven, Michael was able to imagine the transgression—the thrill—it must have been to bring a girl to that place.

"Why were you thinking of Paula Daltrey?" Michael asked.

"You lie here all day, waiting for the doctor to visit, sort of drifting in and out of sleep, and these things just pop into your head."

"Maybe that ball's pushing a button in your brain." He pretended to push a button in the air with his finger. It was a calculated risk.

"Maybe." Connor laughed. "Maybe I'll come out of surgery a genius!"

"My brother the genius!" Michael wanted it to be like this: he and Connor laughing about things, everything not so bad.

"Or maybe I'll come out a vegetable. That could happen, too."

"That won't happen."

Connor nodded gravely, and the back of Michael's eyes burned. The wave of sadness surprised him, not because it was unexpected, but because it was so savage and short-lived. For a moment, Michael was certain that everything was hopeless.

"Do you remember when Mom was here?" Connor asked. "It was this hospital. I'm used to this hospital."

"I was thinking of that." He hadn't been but he felt like he should have been.

"Nobody thought she was going to die, and then she did."

It was a strange thing to say, and Michael opened his mouth slightly. In agreement or disagreement, he wasn't sure.

"All we ever talk about is women," Connor said. He seemed pleased with this statement.   "Even when the woman's our mother."

"Paula Daltrey, though." Connor shook his bald head. "You should remember her."

"I think I remember her."

"No, you'd know."

Connor was right. Michael had decided he couldn't remember Paula Daltrey after all, though he wished he could.

"I'm going to eat this," Michael said, standing and pulling the cheeseburger out of the bag. "If you're not."

Doctor Saramago knocked on the open door before coming in. He was a handsome man with an uncomfortable smile that Michael guessed he wore all day. When he saw

Michael, he extended his hand to him and turned toward
Connor. "The brother?"

"That's what our mother told us."

"Well, you look alike."

Michael felt ridiculous holding the cheeseburger. He
slid it into the bag and moved to the back wall to give his
brother and the doctor space. Doctor Saramago tapped a
clipboard with a pen. Michael thought about the command
in that clipboard; from it, he could see who was going to
make it and who wasn't, whether someone's headaches were
migraines or a tumor. Was it awful, Michael wondered,
to know those things? When patients looked at Doctor
Saramago, did he value being the person who knew what
the result was, how long it was going to be, what the
percentages were?

"You're welcome to stay," Doctor Saramago said. It
took Michael a second to realize the doctor was speaking
to him.

"I should be going." Michael reached for his coat and
the bag. He didn't know if Connor wanted him there or
not. It was easiest to go.

Michael waved to Connor, who lifted his right hand,
and headed for the door. Halfway down the hall, Michael
veered into one of the waiting rooms. He sat, and using
his fingers as beads, began to say a rosary to himself.
But realizing that he was improvising, that he couldn't
remember the procession, he snapped his hand shut and
left for the parking lot.

·

On Monday, the third day, Elaine agreed to come with Michael. "You don't have to do anything special," she said in the hospital elevator. "He appreciates you just being here."

"Just being here," Michael said. "That isn't enough."

She was driving back to Boston the next morning. There was a presentation her office said it couldn't do without her. Earlier at the hotel, Michael had watched her straining on the phone.

"He's very close to me, and it's a serious operation."

Michael was surprised to find the door to Connor's room closed. He looked at Elaine, who shrugged, and knocked twice. There was a muffling of voices inside and a chair leg scraping against tile. When his father opened the door, Michael's first instinct was to ask how his mother was doing.

"We weren't expecting you just yet," his father said.

"What are you doing here?"

"My son is in the hospital. You thought I wouldn't come?"

Michael pushed the door all the way open and stepped into the room. A priest was leaning forward, listening to Connor, who was talking quickly. Michael turned around to look at his father, who clasped his hands in front of him, as if about to enter into a long story. He was even fatter than Michael remembered. Elaine stood in the doorway, unsure of where to go.

"Father McAllister is an old family friend," his father said. "He was happy to come."

"It's all right." Connor was sitting up. "Really, Michael.

Take off your coat."

"You can ask him to leave." Michael gestured at his father. "You can do that."

"Take off your coat. Take Elaine's coat." Connor waved to the doorway.

Michael unzipped his coat but didn't take it off. Elaine squeezed past his father and walked toward Michael. He hadn't seen his father since his mother's funeral. When his mother died, they had little reason to keep in touch. The last time he called Michael was to tell him he was marrying his mistress of ten years. That was two months after the funeral. But Connor was never as resentful. He continued to talk to their father every few weeks and even went to the wedding. Later Connor said, Well how long did she wait?

"If we stand around Connor, we can join in prayer." Father McAllister sounded slightly impatient. Michael wondered how long he'd been here, whether or not he had others to visit in the hospital.

Elaine leaned her face up to Michael's ear. "I can't take the Host," she whispered.

"You can't what?"

She lowered her voice so that it was barely audible. "I can't take the Host, and you shouldn't either. Neither of us has been to Mass in years."

Michael nodded. It hadn't occurred to him that Father McAllister was about to administer the Host, that this was why his father had asked him to come.

After making the Sign of the Cross, Father McAllister began a prayer, and Michael mouthed the words in the distant but respectful way he mouthed the national anthem at baseball games.

Connor and their father prayed with Father McAllister, but their father spoke too loudly, as if to remind the room that he knew the words.

Father McAllister placed his hands on Connor's head. His hands were dark with liver spots, and in contrast, Connor's bald head appeared oddly sleek and youthful. Father McAllister anointed Connor's forehead with oil and took his hands to anoint them, as well. Michael clenched his fists, thinking of how he would sometimes spill olive oil on his hands cooking and rub it off quickly on his jeans.

Father McAllister took out a plain container, not much smaller than a pocket watch, from which he produced the Host. As Father McAllister finished the prayer and placed the Host on Connor's tongue, Michael marveled at how modern the container seemed, at how ordinary and sad the whole ceremony was in a brightly lit hospital room.

How could Michael describe his father's false humility? He held out his tongue like it was a thing he'd never realized he had.

When Father McAllister turned to Elaine, she crossed her arms and hands over her chest, which was a gesture he recognized. Michael did the same, and as Father McAllister lowered his head to put away the container, Connor burst out: "What are you doing?"

"I can't receive," Michael said.

"Are you Buddhist now?"

"I haven't been to Mass in years." Michael looked at Father McAllister. "It isn't right, is it, Father?"

Father McAllister put his hand over his closed
mouth—his index finger touching his nose, his pinky
dangling from his chin—and Michael's father shook his
head sympathetically.

"You're still Catholic," Connor said.

"That isn't the point," Michael said. "I'm not in a state
of grace."

"You must be in a state of grace to receive," Father
McAllister said.

Connor glared at Michael, as if his statement were a
trump card and somehow a betrayal.

"I'm going to leave now," Michael said. "That might be
best."

"That might," Connor agreed.

Michael zipped up his coat. He had expected an
objection and wasn't quite sure what to do with this.

"Take care," Elaine said. She took one of Connor's
hands and gripped it. Michael watched carefully. Connor
didn't grip back. He was angry, or maybe hurt, and Michael
didn't want to leave.

Michael didn't say anything on the walk back to the
car. He moved slowly through the hallways, and when
they got inside the car, Elaine laid her hands flat on the
dashboard and said, "We can stay here for a while. If it
makes you feel better, we can stay."

"What does that even mean: state of grace?"

"It doesn't have to mean anything. It's strange being in
a room like that with a priest. It was strange for me, too."

"You knew what to do." Michael crossed his arms
over his chest. His left elbow bumped the steering wheel.

"Where did you learn that?"

"I don't know. Maybe I saw someone do it once. It's not important."

Michael looked at Elaine. She was staring blankly at her hands, which were dry and tough from the cold. That night, she would rub moisturizer over them from a tube the size of his thumb and remind him that if she didn't, they would bleed. She would have to leave early the next morning. She'd want to go to her apartment first to shower and change her clothes. Really, it would make more sense to leave now, this afternoon, but she wouldn't do that. For him, she would stay. She'd get a wake-up call at five and be gone by five-thirty. She would dress quietly in the dark, wash her face in the bathroom, pull her hair into a ponytail, and lift his head off the pillow to kiss him before she left. What would she think about during the drive? Would she worry over Connor, over him worrying about Connor? Or would she have selfish thoughts—how does this affect me?—and stop herself, actually slam her palm against the steering wheel driving over the Sagamore Bridge, to say, Be more understanding, try to see this from Connor's point of view? This was all just his limited way of thinking. Simple and foolish. A waste of time with his brother a five-minute walk away, maybe imagining this as the last full day of his life.

"I'd like to go to Sandy Neck," Michael said, reaching for Elaine's hand. "It's not far from here."

"All right. We can do that."

Elaine smiled, but Michael could barely understand the reason himself. She reached for her seat belt with her free hand, and just as it clicked into the buckle, he leaned across the car and kissed her.

It was easier, Michael realized, to talk about their father. Easier to marvel with Connor at their father's visit the day before than talk about the obvious. Michael was glad for the drama. He could almost convince himself he was glad his father had come. Anything was better than talking about the surgery. He'd intentionally left his watch at the hotel, but he still knew how much longer it was. He decided on the walk over that he would give his brother the last hour to himself.

"Dad looked like hell, didn't he?" Connor drummed his abdomen with his fingers.

"It wasn't his fighting weight," Michael said.

"He's pushing two-fifty, anyhow."

"I can see straight through you." Michael pointed to Connor's belly, where his fingers were still tapping. When Connor looked down to examine himself, Michael wished he hadn't said it.

"You'll have some steaks to eat when you get out of here."

"You treating? I'll take two."

Michael nodded. He would buy his brother a steak. And if they went to a bar afterward, he would buy the pitchers, smiling when his brother began to feel them. Connor was his younger brother; Michael didn't see how that could change.

"Elaine's coming back tonight. After work. We'll both be here when you come to."

"I like Elaine," Connor said. "I hope you don't think I don't."

"I know you like her."

"I just don't like that she's married."

"You don't like that she's separated."

Connor moved his bald head from side to side. It was an acknowledgment more than a concession. But Michael wasn't offended. He knew that, in a way, Connor meant it politely.

"You should go to Mass again." Connor scratched his nose, and Michael could see that Connor's hand was shaking. "Even if you can't marry, you should go."

"We can marry."

"There's a church in your neighborhood. I looked it up."

"I was thinking deathbed repentance."

"That's dicey."

"Oscar Wilde did it."

"Oscar Wilde did a lot of things. You don't want to play that game with Oscar Wilde."

Michael walked to the bedside table. He hadn't been able to sit since he'd arrived. There was a second bouquet of flowers on the table, and he wondered if his father had brought it, if it had been there the day before. He reached into the bouquet for a card. There wasn't one. The flowers were already dry and faded. "When did you call Dad?" he asked.

"I was loopy when I called him. The tranquilizers, you know."

"I don't mind."

"I'm sorry for the way things went yesterday. It didn't

have to be like that."

"It's all right."

"I've been thinking about things. I wrote a little will."
Connor lifted his book off the table. There was a single
piece of paper underneath it, which he handed to Michael.
"You're in it. You get my good looks."

Michael looked at the paper. In an uneven script,
halfway down the page, Connor had written: *Catholic
burial. In Mom's cemetery, if possible. Use my money.* There
was nothing else on the paper.

"This is ridiculous," Michael said.

"Just be in charge."

Michael folded the paper in fours and placed it in
his back pocket. He knew instantly that the paper was
something he would have for the rest of his life. "You'll be
fine."

"If you'll excuse me, I have an appointment."

"Two steaks. My treat."

Connor held up two fingers, and Michael leaned down
to hug him. Connor's arms felt thin—thinner than they
actually were—and Michael tried to imagine being his
brother.

Their father was in the parking lot when Michael got
back to the hotel. He was leaning against his car like he
wished he were smoking a cigarette.

"What's this?" Michael said as soon as he was close
enough.

"Connor said you were staying here."

"He goes under any minute."

"I meant to stop by." His father coughed into his fist.

"I couldn't bring myself to do it."

"Elaine and I are going later. You can come."

"It's difficult for me. It was difficult with your mother. I still remember that."

Michael tugged at his scarf. The weather had been cold since he'd been on the Cape, and now a sharp wind was rolling empty coffee cups around the parking lot. His father had on a bulky winter coat and hat, though he didn't seem as large against the wide flat plane of asphalt. If his father had apologized right then, Michael would have taken him back. Michael wanted to think that he could read concern on his father's face. He would have been content to read anger or sadness—anything, really—but he couldn't. The truth: His father's face was soft and undoubting, as it had always been. His nose was a little red, which was endearing, though some might have assumed he'd been drinking.

"How long have you been waiting out here?" Michael asked.

"Not long." His father kicked a chunk of brown ice from the underside of his car. "Elaine's staying here. Things must be pretty serious."

"She comes back tonight." It pained Michael to hear his father talk like this, to start the conversations they would have if they kept in touch. Michael briefly considered inviting his father to his room, but he knew he wouldn't come. This was goodbye, now, in the parking lot.

"You be good to her. She looks like your mother."

"She doesn't look like Mom."

"A little around the eyes, maybe."

Michael nodded. He would grant his father that. It was strange to think about how Elaine had never met his mother. She never would.

"I suppose I'm off." His father pulled his keys from his pocket. Even in the cold, his hands looked delicate. Like a priest's, his mother had said.

"Elaine and I will be there later."

"He shouldn't even be there. In terms of brain surgery, Mass General—"

"Offer's on the table."

His father nodded and opened the car door. Every time Michael saw him, Michael wondered if it would be the last. They'd never known what to say to each other, how to act. Even when Michael said goodbye, it sounded like a question.

Michael called Elaine as soon as he got back to the room. Nobody picked up, and he figured she was at a meeting. He'd call in a half-hour, and if she wasn't there, he'd call again. He didn't want to leave a message. He wanted control over his voice.

He was hungry. That was something that never happened with Elaine. It wasn't that she always cooked— they tried to split the cooking—just that she made sure they ate. Michael opened the curtains, thinking he could spot a restaurant within walking distance. He couldn't see anything and he was struck—suddenly and awkwardly— with a longing for Elaine's hair, the teeth in her laugh, her small feet. There were hardly any cars in the parking lot. The clouds sat heavy and low, as if the sky had dropped them.

Michael followed the fence along the perimeter of the parking lot with his eyes. The fence was probably five feet high, and a few tree limbs bent over it, running their crippled fingers through the wind. The creek that cut through the trees had completely frozen over. There were no boys smoking cigarettes this time, no discernible trace that they'd ever been there, and Michael thought of his brother bringing Paula Daltrey to the cranberry bog where they played hockey. He believed Connor that she was beautiful. He saw her with red hair and a wave of freckles across her cheeks that carried over the bridge of her nose. She couldn't skate well but she had her own pair, black and sturdy. She didn't mind the cold at all.

Connor had driven her to the cranberry bog without telling her where they were going. She recognized the road they were taking, but then he made a left she'd never made before, and they came to a series of narrow dirt roads. For a second, she was worried. But Paula trusted him in the confident, thoughtless way that sixteen-year-olds will, and when he pulled off the side of the road beside a pine tree, she was only excited. There was a half-hour of sunlight left, and nobody had ever taken her to a place like this.

For his part, Connor was nervous. He'd suggested they go skating without considering whether or not anyone would be there, and now they were walking toward the bog. He was lucky. The bog was empty, and the ice was thick. It all seemed like an omen, though he didn't believe in things like that.

Paula wasn't used to skating outside and she kept stumbling over the thin patches of snow. Connor smiled to show that he was sympathetic, but mostly he wanted to show off. He was a good skater. She watched his runs and quick turns with a combination of pleasure and annoyance, but when he stopped abruptly and took her hands, she thought to herself: This is something you will remember. Connor did not enjoy the same awareness. He knew only that he had to do something. He skated backward, pulling her with him, and when they began to gain speed, he told her that she had to lead. That he couldn't see what was behind him, and he couldn't slow down. Paula kept her skates close together—more than once her knees banged against each other—and when she told Connor to turn, she bent her body with the turn.

How jarring it must have been when he finally tripped, and she came sprawling over him. How surprising it had to be when, gently lifting her off his chest, he noticed for the first time beneath the ice a faint distant crimson. Michael wondered, did Connor reach over then to show her, or did he give himself time to hold the blur in his head? It must have seemed like there was so much time. The cold hadn't wet his skin yet, and the sun was still trapped among the pines. Beside him a beautiful girl was tightening her laces, while everywhere beneath them, invisible red fish swam indifferent to the ice.